This

Healing

Journey

The Mountain Series

BOOK 12

MISTY M. BELLER

To my son,

A gift from God in every way.

I love you more than you could ever imagine.

And the King shall answer and say unto them, Verily I say unto you, Inasmuch as ye have done it unto one of the least of these my brethren, ye have done it unto me.

Matthew 25:40 (KJV)

Chapter One

On the brink of finally claiming this dream. Why do my fears rise to taunt me now?

~ Nathaniel

JUNE, 1880
NEAR BUTTE, MONTANA TERRITORY

*M*eeting a stranger shouldn't make him so nervous. Shouldn't even give him a second's worry. Nathaniel Peak rubbed a sweating palm down his trouser leg as he tried to settle into his horse's stride. After all, he'd faced down hundreds of enemy rifles and charged into the midst of Indian war cries and brutal spears. By the grace of God he'd survived. Survived and finally escaped the ruthless life in the cavalry he'd grown to hate so fiercely.

Now, a simple life as a civilian rancher shouldn't set his nerves on edge. He was only meeting a neighbor. Maybe a family. These were the people living nearest his new homestead. The neighbors he could call on for help and return the favor in kind.

Yet, since the rising sun had awakened him that morning, he'd had a gnawing in his gut. The feeling that came before battle, the sting of goose flesh and hair standing on end. But why?

It wasn't as if these landowners were more important than others he'd met in his life. He was making too much of this introduction in his mind, but he couldn't seem to squelch the anxiety.

To his left, the trees parted to reveal a majestic view of distant mountain peaks rising up as far as he could see. *This* was why he'd chosen to locate his ranch here. Views like that stirred something deep inside him, making him come alive in a way he wanted to feel for the rest of his days.

To the right, a worn path turned off the main trail, and he reined his mare that direction, toward the spire of smoke rising above the trees. Would these be a pair of grizzled mountain men who'd teamed up to make their work a bit easier for themselves? Or a young couple trying to make a go of life in these majestic mountains, where a man could work his own land and appreciate the fruits of his labors?

As the trees gave way to an open clearing, the cabin sitting in the middle proved to be the source of the rising chimney smoke. A dog barked then bounded from the porch toward him. A big white wooly animal who showed a pair of snarling teeth as it neared.

"Hey, there." Nathaniel kept his horse moving forward steadily, careful to make sure his posture didn't show any hint of threat toward the canine. Nor any fear.

A sound from the cabin porch brought his focus up to where a man stepped outside. He paused at the top of the stairs, a hat shadowing his face so it was hard to get a read on his age and demeanor. The dog loped back to the porch and took its position beside the man.

Nathaniel stopped his horse about fifteen strides away from the structure. Near enough they could speak without yelling, but far enough he didn't appear to be pushing his way in uninvited.

He raised a hand. "Howdy."

The other man nodded, lifting a matching palm in greeting. "We don't see many new faces around here." His voice sounded friendly enough.

Nathaniel forced away a bit of his nerves as he tipped up the brim of his hat so the fellow could get a clear look at him. "I'm homesteading the land to the east of you." He pointed in the direction of his property. "There's an old trapper's cabin I've been staying in. Maybe you've seen the place. Anyway, thought I'd come introduce myself. Nathaniel Peak."

"Glad to meet you." The man stepped down the stairs and moved toward him. "I'm Reuben Scott. Come in and stay a bit. My wife'll have coffee on and biscuits made fresh this morning."

Nathaniel eased out a breath as he dismounted. He turned to Scott and extended a hand to meet the outstretched grip. "I'd appreciate that." An invitation to breakfast was almost better than he could have hoped. He

9

could address business now without having to come back a second time.

He tied his horse at the hitching post to the right of the stairs, then fell into step beside Reuben Scott, glancing around the clearing at the barn, corrals, and a few other outbuildings. "Looks like a nice place you have here."

Not luxurious, to be sure, but well-equipped for a quiet mountain ranch. It would take some doing to get his own cluster of ramshackle buildings up to this level of simple efficiency. All the structures here seemed well-maintained.

On the porch, Scott motioned to the dog to stay out, then pushed open the door and stepped inside first. "We've a visitor." His words were directed to someone within, then he cleared the opening and waved for Nathaniel to enter.

As he stepped into the interior, he squinted to catch the surroundings while his eyes adjusted to the dimmer lighting. Sound to his right drew his focus.

A woman stood over a cookstove, a table to her back. She replaced the lid on a pot and turned to him with a smile. "Welcome."

Reuben Scott moved near her, then pointed to Nathaniel. "This is our new neighbor to the east, Nathaniel Peak. He's taken the old hunting cabin."

She clasped her hands together as joy lit her pretty face. "Wonderful. I'm Cathleen Scott." She motioned toward the table. "Sit and visit. I'll pour coffee."

Either these two were starved for human interaction, or they were genuinely pleasant people. Whichever the case, he stepped toward the table and sank into a ladder-back chair on the long side. Reuben took one at the head.

"Are you new to the area?" The man leaned back in his seat, crossing his arms in a comfortable pose.

"Mostly. I just finished four years in the 2nd US Calvary Regiment, B Troop. We rode through here a couple times, and I remembered it being one of the prettiest countries I'd ever seen. As soon as I could get away from the fighting, I made my way back."

He watched Reuben's face as he spoke and didn't miss the way his eyes seemed to close off, although his expression didn't harden. Did this man feel the same way about the Indian wars? Or did he have another reason to dislike the cavalry?

Mrs. Scott placed mugs in front of each of them—ceramic, not the tin he was so accustomed to. He glanced at her face but saw nothing there except kind civility.

Perhaps this was a good time to ease the conversation away from himself. Turning back to the man, he took a sip of the warm brew. The liquid eased down without a hint of bitterness. "Ah, that's good. Shouldn't even carry the same name as the sludge we drank in the regiment."

Reuben's jaw tightened at the word *regiment*. The man clearly disliked something about the cavalry—a sentiment Nathaniel shared with him. Maybe if he told of his reasons for leaving, they could find common ground with better footing.

He set the mug on the table and met the man's gaze. "I signed on to the cavalry back in Virginia, the same as my

11

father had done, and his father before him. It was my mother's greatest wish that I follow in their footsteps and protect my country on horseback. Within days, I was assigned to the 2nd Regiment and sent westward with a group of other new troopers. What I found when I arrived was nothing like what I expected."

He stared into his mug as those early days came back to him. "The Indians. I..." How did he say this without seeming overly harsh toward his superiors? Not all had been heartless. For many, this was simply a war they'd been commanded to win. Yet war should never be waged against women and children.

Swallowing, he did his best to sum up the story in as few words as possible. "I suppose you could say I didn't always agree with the methods we were commanded to use in fulfilling our orders. For that matter, I struggled with why there was such a need to keep the Indians confined to reservations in the first place. In many ways, it seems possible and better for us all to settle in together doing what the Bible says. 'As much as possible, live peaceably with all men.'" He scrubbed a hand through his hair. "I suppose soldiering wasn't the best line of work for me."

He chanced a look at Reuben. He'd never bared his soul so thoroughly to strangers. What would the man say? He'd not meant to put him on the spot nor dive into such weighty matters in the first five minutes of conversation. Perhaps it was best they change the subject now.

Reuben's jaw had softened, and his mouth curved in a hint of a smile. "I couldn't have said it better myself. The part about living peaceably that is." Then he reached a hand forward. It took Nathaniel a second for his stunned mind to realize what the man offered.

He took the extended hand, accepting the friendship locked firmly in the grip. Reuben's gaze settled in his, something like respect shimmering in his dark eyes.

Then the man eased back in his chair with a comfortable sigh. "Now tell us, what do you need to help you settle in? That shack's not been lived in regularly for a while. You need a hand to make the place habitable?"

Mrs. Scott placed a plate of fluffy biscuits on the table, along with butter and some kind of jam. He'd meant only a glance at the food, but the aroma didn't do the fare justice. He could almost taste the warm melding of sweet flavors, even though it had been years since he'd enjoyed such bliss. Not since he joined the cavalry.

A chuckle drifted from Reuben as the man nudged the plate toward him. "Go ahead. Eat. Cathleen makes better biscuits than anyone I know. Even better than my mum's."

"Speaking of Mum, I think I hear her waking." Mrs. Scott spoke for the first time since they'd sat at the table. The swish of her skirts sounded as she moved toward the doors against the back wall.

Reuben watched his wife go, a glimmer in his eyes most married men seemed to lose after the courting days. Then he turned his focus back to Nathaniel. "Mum doesn't remember much these days. It might confuse her to meet you. She'll be polite, but she may think you're someone she once knew."

Nathaniel nodded. "Getting old isn't easy." He couldn't withstand the call of the biscuits any longer but tried not to make a fanfare of scooping one onto his plate.

Reuben did the same, and an easy quiet settled as they loaded the bread with extras. The first bite was heavenly, even better than he'd imagined.

"So you didn't say how we could help. I'm sure Cathy will want to send food with you."

He'd wanted an opening to state his main purpose for coming here, but he had to pull himself from the warm biscuits to answer. "Actually, I'm looking to buy stock. Cattle and good horseflesh if I can find it. My plan is to raise mostly horses, but the cattle will help offset the lean times. Do you know the best places in this area to buy healthy animals?"

Reuben's gaze drifted into the distance as he chewed, his mind likely far away. "I don't mind selling you a few of our cattle, but our herd's still low from when I had to trade some to O'Hennessey last year. He may have more to part with than we do. I know he has a few horses, but I'm not sure if any will be what you're looking for." He turned back to Nathaniel. "He's our neighbor to the west, about an hour's ride. I can go over there with you if you'd like."

Nathaniel tried to keep the grin from spreading too wide on his face. "I'd appreciate that."

A clanging sounded from the back chamber. At the same time the dog growled on the porch outside. Reuben's head cocked, then he pushed to his feet and moved toward the small window at the far end of the room.

Nathaniel stood, too. Had someone else come to visit? He wouldn't expect many people this far up in the mountains. Reuben's face looked troubled as he peered through the glass, then he stepped to the rear door his wife had entered. When he poked his head inside what must be a bed chamber, the hum of voices sounded, but not loud enough for Nathaniel to make out words.

He kept his place by the table, waiting to see where he was needed. Reuben strode toward the front door, then paused as if just remembering Nathaniel was there. He waved toward the porch. "Three unfamiliar riders. You can come meet them too. Maybe we have more new neighbors."

Nathaniel followed him out, but couldn't summon the light spirit the man's words tried to relay. Maybe because Reuben's face held a seriousness that matched the foreboding in his own chest.

Chapter Two

As much as I long for the happiness of those dearest, I can't help but wonder if I'll ever find my own place.

~ Hannah

Hannah Grant reined her horse alongside her mother's mare, letting her father's tall, broad shoulders lead the way on his paint. The farmyard they rode into was tidy—almost cozy, surrounded by trees as it was. Grass grew in even patches, split by footpaths from the house to the barn and each of the outbuildings, a sign that the inhabitants didn't allow the stock to overgraze the clearing. Was her half-brother responsible for this sensible management? Or had he long ago left this place, the home of his birth?

How long would they need to search before finding Reuben Scott?

A fluffy white dog barked as it bounded off the porch toward them. It was larger than Mustang, their dog back in Canada. In fact, it was closer to the size of Grizz, Uncle Daniel's dog, who lived in the cabin beside their own.

Her father rarely showed nerves, but she could feel the tension emanating from his straight posture as they advanced toward the cabin. This must be hard on him, reuniting with the son he'd given up at birth. She'd heard only a few details, but every time he spoke of his lost twins, his eyes took on a sadness that made her want to crawl in his lap and hug the pain away.

The cabin's door opened, and a man stepped out. Then a second stranger. Neither was old enough to be Quinn Scott, the person who'd raised her father's son. In fact, both looked to be nearer her own twenty-four years, or a little older.

Her pulse thumped harder in her chest. Was one of them her brother?

The first man stepped to the edge of the porch as they neared, but a hat shielded his face in shadows. The dog trotted back to the porch and took its place beside what must be its master.

Papa reined in and slid to the ground, dropping his reins so his horse would stand quiet. He didn't have to tell her and her mother to stay put. This was *his* moment if one of these turned out to be his son. He would invite her and Mama in when he was ready.

He stepped forward until only a half dozen strides separated him from the porch. Neither of the younger men had spoken, as though they could feel the weight of the meeting.

17

"Hello." Papa's voice eased out in its normal rich cadence. "I'm Simeon Grant. Is Quinn Scott here, by chance?"

The man nearest the stairs straightened. The words seemed to affect him, but was his reaction strong enough to prove he recognized her father's name?

He responded in a clear, strong voice. "My father passed away a couple years ago. I'm Reuben Scott. Can I help you with something?"

Her breath caught in her lungs, and the gasp beside her proved her mother's reaction was much the same.

This was *Reuben*.

She couldn't see Papa's face, but he did a remarkable job of keeping his reaction from showing in his posture. Would he reveal himself now?

He took a step closer, his voice dropping, yet she could still hear his strong tenor. "I'm sorry to hear that. What of Mrs. Scott, his wife?"

"My mother is here, although her memory fails her more often than not. Did my parents know you well?"

A bead of silence hung before Papa answered. "Our acquaintance wasn't long, but it meant a great deal to me. And I think to them also." A vague answer, but still very true.

Reuben stared at her father for a long moment. Maybe taking his measure? Possibly debating within himself whether it was wise to invite them in.

At last, he straightened, and his gaze roamed over all three of them. "If you'd like to come in, you can see Mum for

18

a few minutes. Don't be surprised if she doesn't remember you. Some days, she doesn't seem to recognize even me."

Papa's face looked stoic as he turned back to help her mother dismount. A kindness she surely didn't need, as Mama was as capable in the saddle as any ranch hand. But he always offered, and she always accepted. Maybe more for the kiss he usually stole when her feet touched the ground than anything else.

This time, he didn't attempt a kiss, but Hannah couldn't miss the lingering gaze between them. So much they could say to each other without words, it sometimes brought a lump to her throat. Would she ever find a man who loved her with the same strength her parents felt toward each other?

She certainly wouldn't find such a man hidden away in the Canadian mountain wilderness where she'd spent her life. Thus the reason she'd begged to come on this journey.

As they secured their horses to the hitching post, the second man who'd hung back near the cabin door seemed to be taking his leave. Now that she could see him better, his features drew her attention more than they should. He was young indeed, but he carried himself with a crisp efficiency and confidence many older men didn't possess.

As he strode down the stairs, his gaze slid toward her family, snagging on her. She dropped her focus back to her horse, stroking its neck. But that look—that connection—had shaken her more than it should. Was she so starved for male attention that any stranger would do?

19

As that man mounted his horse and rode away, she followed her parents onto the porch, where Papa introduced her and Mama. Reuben nodded. His blue eyes were different in coloring from Papa's brown, yet their intensity felt much the same. His height and the breadth of his shoulders was similar, too. How could anyone not recognize their connection?

Did Reuben know? If not, she could only imagine the shock this would be. *Lord, guide our time here.*

Reuben motioned for the dog to stay outside, then they followed the man into the cozy cabin, a little smaller than their own. He pointed to chairs by the hearth at the far end of the room. "Mum will be most comfortable in her rocking chair, but take any of the other seats. I'll bring her out." He turned and stepped through one of the two doors in the back wall.

Papa didn't move, didn't step toward the chairs. Just stood, his gaze locked on the well-worn rocker. Did he remember it from before? She could only imagine the pain resurrected from seeing this place again.

Actually, she couldn't imagine.

Her father had been her strength through all her growing up years, completely devoted to their family and not afraid to show his pleasure in being with them. She'd heard his circumstances had been dire when he'd given Reuben and his twin sister to the Scott family to raise. It had been before he'd met Mama, and the twins' mother had died just after their birth.

But still, for Papa to give up his offspring—*his family*—she couldn't fathom it.

Mama slipped her hand into his, always there as silent support.

The bed chamber door opened, and Reuben stepped out leading an older woman by the hand. She looked to be in her early sixties, although her hair had already faded to a pure white that made her seem a decade older.

Or maybe it was the vacant look in her faded blue eyes that aged her. She clutched Reuben's hand as she shuffled into the room, and another woman followed, holding her other hand. This lady was younger, closer to Hannah's age, with striking auburn hair and regal features.

Reuben motioned to the younger woman. "This is my wife, Cathleen." Then he walked the older woman to the rocking chair and eased her into the seat.

Finally, he straightened and motioned her father forward. "I'll introduce you."

Papa stepped close until he stood in front of the older lady alongside Reuben. So close, the similarity between them was unmistakable. Both men held that capable, frontiersman look, something she could hardly define. A combination of power and lean strength, coupled with quiet wisdom. Her other brothers, William and Robert, possessed the same, although it looked a little different on them. Maybe the quality was simply not as seasoned.

Reuben still held the older woman's hand, and he spoke to her now. "Mum, an old friend came to visit you. Do you remember Simeon Grant?"

Papa dropped down to sit on his haunches so he was eye level with the woman. "Hello, Mrs. Scott. I'm glad to see you again. Do you remember many years ago when you helped my wife and me? Our twins were being born, and you brought us into your home and managed the birthing. You were a godsend to us." His voice almost cracked on those last words.

Hannah's chest ached, but she turned her focus from her father to the little woman, who rested her head against the rocker and eased forward and back as she studied him. "I'm glad I was able to help you, honey." Her voice held a wavering quality, as though she didn't have the strength to steady it.

Papa cleared his throat. "It's been thirty years, so I'm sure I've aged a bit. Do you...remember me at all?"

She'd never heard so much desperate hope in her father's voice. The sound made her want to drop to her knees beside the older lady and plead for her to think harder. *Lord, help her recall.*

The woman rocked a moment longer, her eyes fixed on Papa's face. "Honey, we have so many travelers come through here, it's hard for me to keep the faces and names straight. What did you say your name was?"

Papa cleared his throat again, bringing back his usual steady tone. "Simeon Grant."

Another pause as the woman thought. "Seems like that name's familiar. I just can't recall." Her words dragged on with a languid quality that required more patience than Hannah's nerves contained.

22

Papa breathed out a long breath, then looked up at Reuben. Slowly, he rose to standing. "I suppose I'll need to tell you everything then. I was hoping she could help. Do you have a few minutes to sit?"

Reuben shot a glance to his wife, who stood on the other side of the rocker, then looked back at Papa and motioned toward the other chairs by the fire. "Have a seat."

They brought three more chairs from around the dining table, and it didn't take long for everyone to settle. Reuben sat beside the older Mrs. Scott, with his wife on his other side. Papa positioned himself directly opposite Reuben, with Mama close by.

Hannah sat at the edge of the group in one of the ladder-back chairs. She almost wished she were nearer the elderly woman so she'd have someone's hand to clutch when the conversation grew tense.

As it surely would.

Everyone looked at Papa, waiting for him to take the lead. His face held its usual calm steadiness. There was no sign he was nervous about the coming conversation. His gaze slid from Reuben to his adopted mother, then back to Reuben. "About thirty years ago, I was traveling through this country with my first wife, Nora. We'd purchased some land another week's ride into the mountains and planned to build a house there, but Nora was with child, and her time came much sooner than we expected. Her pains had started, and I still remember how relieved I was when we saw the smoke from this chimney through the trees." He motioned toward the hearth—cold at the moment, since only the cookstove fire was needed in June.

"Mrs. Scott realized what was happening right away and brought Nora in to their bed to have the baby." He motioned to the two doors along the back wall. "The birthing felt like it took hours, and I could tell Nora was wearing down, but I thought that must be normal. Mrs. Scott seemed to have it all in hand, knowing exactly what to do."

Hannah shot a glance at Mrs. Scott to see if Papa's words had brought the memories back to her. The woman was looking at him, but her faded eyes didn't seem to register his story. In fact, her expression seemed almost stoic.

"Finally, our little boy was born. So little, yet full of lusty wails. Mrs. Scott wrapped him in a blanket, then handed him to me. I didn't know what to do with such a tiny thing, but he was absolutely perfect."

Papa looked down at his clasped hands as though lost in the memories of holding the infant—his firstborn son. Then his hands gripped tighter, his knuckles going white. "The labor pains kept coming though." He looked up, his eyes hollow. "A second baby was on its way. A girl. She was even smaller than the boy." He turned his large, calloused hand palm up. "Not much bigger than my hand."

It wasn't hard to imagine a sweet babe, skin pale and pinkened, lying in her father's work-worn grip.

His Adam's apple bobbed as he seemed to be working to hold himself together. "I was trying to feed the baby boy warm milk to ease his crying while your mama held the little girl. I didn't realize how bad things were with

24

Nora." His throat worked again, and he kept his focus on his palm. "Until just before she slipped away."

A long moment passed without a word. Hannah's chest ached so much it was hard to breathe, much less speak.

At last, her father raised his head to take in the three sitting across from him. Reuben's face was void of any expression, as though protecting himself from the tale unfolding. But his wife had pressed a hand over her mouth, her eyes glimmering with emotion.

Papa pressed on with his story. "I was so deep in my grief, I barely knew what happened those next few days. Mr. and Mrs. Scott handled most of the care for the babes, and I finally pulled myself free enough to realize I had to make a plan.

"We had no home where we were going, only virgin trees and mountains I'd never actually seen. And winter was coming fast. The trip had taken much longer than we'd thought—such a young, foolish thing I was. I couldn't imagine how I would be able to care for those two tiny babes. So fragile."

He inhaled a breath that heaved his shoulders. "And even the thought of moving forward without Nora—trying to carry on with the life we'd imagined—I couldn't fathom it.

"The Scotts said they'd be happy to take the children in, to raise them as their own. They'd wanted babies for years but had never been blessed with them. I could see how well they took to the infants already. I barely knew how to feed them. And I knew nothing of what to do if either of those tiny bodies took sick."

He paused again, then leveled his gaze on Reuben, but the younger man met the look with an impassive stare. "I finally realized that the best thing for both babies was for them to stay with the Scotts. But before I left, they promised to write and tell me how the children were doing. They also allowed me to name them. Nora and I had already talked about the names." Papa paused here, took a deep breath. Then, with the same courage he'd used to start the story, he finished it. "Reuben for a boy. The little girl, she looked so much like her mama, I called her by the same. Little Nora."

Reuben's face was blank. Impossible to read. He had to know what Papa's story meant. Had he heard any of it before? Had the Scotts given him any inkling he wasn't their child by birth?

A long silence settled over the room. Thick. Heavy with all the thoughts unspoken. Should they offer to leave and give Reuben and his family time to come to terms with the news?

Before she could think exactly what should be done next, Reuben stood. "Maybe you folks would like coffee and biscuits. I'm going out to check on the stock in the barn." He laid a hand on his wife's shoulder as he walked by, and she reached up to touch his. A simple gesture, but telling. Something Hannah's parents would have done to show silent support in the midst of such a shock.

Chapter Three

Who would have thought that life as I know it could shatter in the space of a quarter hour? I can only cling to the Foundation I know won't shake.

~ Reuben

ension clung to the air as the door closed behind Reuben. Hannah forced a breath out. What could she say to lessen the strain?

The younger Mrs. Scott offered a kind smile and rose from her chair. "It might be easier to eat at the table, but you're welcome to sit where you're most comfortable."

Hannah's parents looked like they might need a moment alone, so she stood to help. She'd much rather be doing something than watching anyway. As she approached her new sister-in-law, she offered a tentative smile. "Tell me how I can help."

Mrs. Scott returned the smile as she pulled a plate of biscuits from the warming oven. "I don't think I caught your name. Mine is Cathleen."

"Hannah. Hannah Grant." She stepped forward to take the biscuits.

Cathleen motioned to the table. "There's already butter and strawberry jam on the table from when we were visiting with our new neighbor. We have a bit of coffee left in the pot, but I'll make more so there's enough to go around. Cups are on the shelf behind that curtain." She pointed toward a pretty calico fabric hanging above the counter.

It felt good to finally have something to do, and they soon had a pleasant snack set out. Her parents brought the extra chairs back to the table, and Cathleen took a plate to the older woman in her rocking chair.

When she returned, Mama said, "Would she like to sit with us?"

It did feel odd to leave the older Mrs. Scott sitting so far apart from the group.

Cathleen gave a sad smile. "We bring her to the table for meals, but she's really more comfortable in her chair. New faces seem to tire her quickly, so it will be good for her to have time alone." She motioned toward the chairs. "Please, sit. You must be exhausted from traveling."

As they ate, Cathleen proved a gracious hostess, asking about their home and how far they'd journeyed. Papa was mostly silent, so Hannah and her mother carried the conversation. It wasn't hard to like this woman, although the weight of Papa's story seemed to hover around them all.

At last, the sound of boots thudded on the porch, and the front door opened. Reuben stepped inside, and once again she was struck by how much he looked like a younger version of her father.

His step was quiet and his manner reserved as he approached the table. "I imagine you've traveled quite a ways, so you're welcome to stay the night if you don't mind pallets on the floor. I've made three stalls ready for your horses."

Not a word about the life-changing news, but that was probably to be expected. Sometimes men handled things like this differently than women would. But at least he wasn't sending them away at gunpoint. Surely he just needed time to adjust.

Papa eased his chair back and stood. "Appreciate that. I'll get the animals settled if you'll show me where."

She itched to go along and help, but the two probably needed a few minutes together. Time to get to know each other. To lower the wall that had been built between them by distance and the passing of time.

Trust would surely come hard for this new brother of hers.

Thoughts churned inside Reuben Scott as he rose from the evening meal later that night. Conversation around the table had been simple. Lightweight.

He still couldn't wrap his mind around the story this man had told. Simeon had even known Nora's name, his tiny twin sister who had died at the age of six months. If the man's story wasn't true, he must have at least known Reuben's parents in past days.

Could this stranger be his father? Reuben had always thought it unusual that he'd grown so tall, even though his mother was a little sprite of a thing and Pa possessed only average height.

But Simeon Grant not only matched his own build, he exceeded it. As they'd walked to the barn earlier, his mind still numb from the consequences of what the man had said, Simeon strode just ahead of him. Seeing his broad shoulders, the way he carried himself—he'd looked at the same so many times in the mirror Cathleen kept in their bed chamber. Even the shape and intensity of the man's eyes were like looking at his own reflection, although the coloring was different.

Why had his parents never told him?

He glanced at his mother, still sitting in her place at the table, wadding a serviette with her bony fingers. Cathleen usually took her into the bed chamber to prepare her for sleep while he saw to the night chores, but perhaps this would be a good time for him to talk with Mum alone.

He moved around to her chair. "Let's go get you settled for bed, Mum."

Cathleen raised her gaze from where she was gathering used plates and dishes. Her eyes showed that well of understanding that always made him so thankful God had brought her to him. She could comprehend his thoughts without him saying a word.

As he helped his mother to her feet, Cathleen turned her sunny smile on their visitors. "Let me just put these to soak, and I'll pull out blankets for your bedding."

Both Mrs. Grant and her daughter—his half-sister?— stood and began clearing the table.

Simeon had already risen, his intense presence almost intimidating with so many people in the small cabin. "I'll bring in more wood. Can I get you water, too?" His question was directed to Cathleen, and she responded with a gracious answer. It looked as if she'd have plenty of help without him.

Mum seemed to shuffle slower than normal as they made their way to her bed chamber. He did his best not to let his own angst rush her.

In the privacy of her room, he looked around the space. What all did Cathleen do with her? Just help her into her nightdress? His wife was so good with Mum, a natural nurse. Not surprising since her father had been an apothecary and both her brothers were doctors in Butte.

Mum reached for a nightdress laid over the chair, and he helped her transition from her day clothes to the simple cotton gown. She picked up a hair comb from her dresser, then sank into a chair. Clearly, she knew the routine better than he did.

He settled on the bed across from her. What was the best way to ease into this conversation? Maybe simply to ask questions that would stir the memories. "Mum, do you remember the day Nora and I were born?"

Her gnarled fingers worked the braid loose from her hair as she studied him. Her eyes seemed to always hold a faraway look these days, but maybe she was thinking back. "Nora?"

He nodded. "My twin sister. Do you remember the day we were born? Was it in the room next door?" His parents had occupied that larger chamber until after his father died and Mum's dementia set in so strongly. Just before he married Cathleen, they'd moved Mum into this smaller room.

That last question seemed to stymie her, and her thin brows lowered in a confused frown. "The room next door?"

He shouldn't have added that detail. Especially since she still went into the wrong bed chamber at times. He leaned forward and propped his elbows on his knees. "When Nora and I were born. Which of us came out first? Do you remember?"

Now that he thought about it, Mum had never really talked about their birth. Wasn't it common for mothers to reminisce about the special details of their children's first minutes? Even the Bible spoke of the unique way the twins Jacob and Esau were born.

She gave him a loving smile. "Oh, honey, you were born before your sister. Such a strong, strapping lad you were. And hungry from your first few minutes."

Those details—sparse though they were—matched what Simeon had said. Except Mum spoke as though she'd been the one giving birth, didn't she? Maybe she hadn't said

32

that specifically. Perhaps he should come directly to the point and ask her.

Steeling his nerves, he worked to find the right words. "Mum, did you give birth to Nora and me, or did our blood parents give us to you and Pa to raise us?"

That confused look came again. Not so much like she was shocked that he'd ask such a thing, but more like she was trying to remember. Had she perpetrated the lie for so many years, she'd forgotten the truth?

At last, her face shifted into another loving smile. "I prayed and prayed for you. And I was so thankful God gave me my little boy and girl. But my Nora..." Her hands slipped to clutch each other in her lap. "My Nora's in heaven. I had so little time with her." She began rocking in her seat, red filling her eyes.

He'd not meant to upset her so. Rising, he moved closer and patted her shoulder. "It's all right, Mum. Nora's in heaven, but I'm here. Everything's all right." He hated feeling so incapable when a woman he loved cried.

She patted his hand as she sniffed. "You're a good son."

He should probably get her in bed before he did or said something else wrong. Maybe she'd be able to answer more questions later, but he'd push no further this night.

Simeon Grant thumbed through the letters again as he knelt by his pack the next morning. Why had he waited so long before coming to find his son? If he'd come just a few years earlier, both Quinn and Ellen would have been alive and in their right minds, able to explain to Reuben the truth of his past.

But would they have?

He'd agreed when he rode away thirty years ago that the Scotts could raise his twins as their own. He hadn't realized at the time that they wouldn't even tell the babes they'd been born to other parents. But maybe that had been best for the children.

Best for Reuben anyway, because tiny, sweet Nora hadn't lived past her first six months.

That old familiar ache tightened his chest again. After he gave Reuben these letters, he'd go visit his first wife's grave. And maybe their baby daughter had been buried alongside the mother who nurtured her in the womb and gave her life with her own last breaths.

He swallowed down the sting of emotion in his throat, then pushed to his feet.

The women had all gone berry picking or something like that. It appeared Reuben had found a good wife in Cathleen, and the love between them was easy to see. *Lord, let him be as happy as Emma and I have been.*

Even with the challenges of their remote life, even with the two babies they'd lost in the early years, Emma was God's gift to him. His second chance, standing by his side as they'd built their home and family.

He pushed to his feet and headed toward the door. The *thwack* of an ax rang through the clearing, coming from the woods to the right of the house. He strode toward the sound and, as he made his way through the trees, saw Reuben's form hacking at the base of a massive trunk.

Mayhap he was trying to vent his frustrations on the poor elm. Should Simeon allow him time alone?

He would just deliver the letters, then leave Reuben to sort things on his own. When his son was ready, he'd be around to talk. Hopefully that would be soon and they could stay on in Reuben's home to get to know him better. But if Simeon, Emma, and Hannah had to take up residence for a while in the nearby town of Butte, they'd do it. Making things right with Reuben—restoring some kind of relationship between them—was more important than he could put words to.

Simeon let his tread ring loudly through the woods so he didn't startle Reuben. His son didn't stop swinging mighty strokes into the trunk, even when Simeon stood near him.

At last, Reuben lowered the tool, his breath coming in and out with a hard rhythm. He didn't look at Simeon, just kept his gaze on the tree. "I've been wanting to pipe water in from the creek so Cathleen doesn't have to haul buckets. I'd like to order metal pipes, but it'd cost a small fortune to get them up here. Elm will have to do."

An ambitious project, to be sure, boring out the center of trees this long. Simeon scanned the area. "Do you have enough trees to reach?"

Reuben pointed at the felled trunk. "If I could find one more elm this length, I think I'd have enough to reach. Unfortunately, the only other elm I've found isn't near as tall."

Simeon raised his eyes to the heavens, taking in the expansive height of this tree. His son had chosen well. Then he scanned the woods around them. "I've bored hemlock to use as pipe before. Do you have any of those around here?"

Reuben cocked his chin. "I don't know it."

"It's an evergreen. Needles look like a fir, but the tree's much taller and scrawnier. I've seen it mostly in the lowlands though." He propped his hands on his hips as he scanned the area once more. "I don't see any around here."

Reuben hoisted the ax again. "Guess I'll have to keep looking for another elm."

Simeon reached for the tool. "Let me have a few swings."

His son didn't hand it over but finally looked at him. In fact, he looked him up and down, as though assessing whether or not such an old fellow was capable of the work.

Simeon raised his brows. "I'm not so old I can't swing an ax."

Reuben dipped his chin, handing over the implement like an offered gift. "Have at it."

As he swung the blade into the tree's wedge, the effort felt good through his travel-worn muscles. Robert and William, his younger sons, handled most of the firewood chopping these days, but his body hadn't forgotten how to swing a finely sharpened ax.

After a while, Simeon handed the ax back to Reuben while he caught his breath. They worked back and forth like that until they'd felled the tree and cut off most of the branches.

Laboring alongside his son—alongside Reuben, at long last—was a special event he'd thought he'd never experience. Yet still, there was an underlying tension, a strain that seemed to drive the man hard.

Cathleen brought plates of her fresh biscuits and roasted meat partway through their work, but Reuben scarcely stopped long enough to swallow down the food.

When he'd cut the last of the branches away from the elm's scarred length, Reuben finally lowered the ax and leaned against it, gazing around. Simeon was moving branches into a pile, separating them by size according to how each would be used. He stopped to rest when Reuben did, mostly so he could hear anything his son would say.

"I suppose I need to get started on evening chores." Reuben picked up the ax and hoisted it onto his shoulder. "I'll cut up the branches another day."

Simeon nodded. He could come back tomorrow and work on them if Reuben didn't need him for anything else. He followed his son back through the trees toward the cabin.

When they reached the clearing, Reuben slowed enough for him to come alongside.

Simeon took the opportunity to talk like he'd been wanting to. "I think Cathleen said you've a herd of cattle, too?"

Reuben nodded. "Not as many anymore. Almost thirty head."

"Sounds like us. About thirty cattle and a handful of horses. That's a nice colt you have in the corral. Mama and baby both."

Reuben's gaze lifted toward the barn and fence they were approaching. "Tashunka always throws good foals. She's worth her weight in gold."

Tashunka. Sounded like an Indian word, maybe Apsaalooke. Did his son have friends among the Indians? There was so much he didn't know about this man. But, though he was eager to question him, better to take things slowly. He had a feeling if he pushed Reuben with anything more than surface enquiries, he'd back away. His son would have to open up when he was ready.

Simeon could only pray he'd still be around when that happened.

Chapter Four

Something doesn't feel right. Are these my instincts, or only my inability to adjust to life as a civilian?

~ Nathaniel

As Nathaniel rode into the Scotts' farmyard the next morning, he scanned the clearing for signs he wasn't too early. Several horses milled in the corral, so hopefully that meant the morning chores were finished.

Reuben had offered to ride with him to look at their neighbor's cattle today, but in the hurry of his other unexpected visitors, they'd not set a time. If the man wasn't ready, Nathaniel would find a way to make himself helpful around the place.

As he neared the porch, the cabin door opened and a woman stepped out. Not Mrs. Scott.

No, this was the younger woman who'd arrived as he was leaving two days before. She was carrying a bucket toward the side edge of the porch until she caught sight of him and froze.

Recognition took only a couple of seconds to dawn on her face, for which he was grateful. He certainly didn't want to frighten her.

He tipped his hat as he reined in his horse. "Hello, ma'am. Is Mr. Scott around?"

She nodded. "Of course." With two quick steps she reached the edge of the porch and dumped the water from her pail onto the ground below, then turned and strode back to the door. Just before she moved back inside, she turned a smile on him that lit her pretty face so it almost stole his breath. Then she turned and disappeared in the house.

He eased out a long exhale. *Settle yourself, Peak. The last thing you need right now is a woman.* As he dismounted, he pictured a herd of cattle spread across the grassy bottom stretch of his land. Horses scattered around the bovine, with long-legged foals running and bouncing between the mares.

That scene was exactly what he had to focus on. No distractions, just a long awaited dream that was finally on the verge of coming to life. He no longer had to bide his time for his term of service in the cavalry to end. All that was required now was solid hard work.

Reuben Scott stepped out from the cabin as he was tying his horse to the hitching rail.

Nathaniel offered a salute. "I know we'd said today, but we didn't agree on a time. If I'm too early, just put me to work." As he offered a smile to soften the words, memory of the pretty lady who'd just been on the porch slipped in. Maybe Reuben was too busy with his visitors.

He quickly added, "Or if this is a bad time, I can go on my own." He'd sure rather have this new friend along with him, but he could stand on his own two feet as well as the next man.

Reuben glanced toward the barn. "Today works. Let me just throw hay out for the horses and saddle my own." The man turned back toward the cabin door, then paused. "You, uh, wanna come in for coffee? The cabin's a bit crowded just now, but one more body won't make a difference if you don't mind."

Nathaniel shifted from one foot to the other. He wasn't particularly fond of a room full of people himself, as much as he'd like to lay eyes on that pretty lady a final time.

Better he stay put, though.

"'Preciate the offer, but I'm filled up for now." Even as he spoke the words, the smooth taste of Mrs. Scott's coffee wove its way through his memory. He could taste it, even after two days.

Reuben nodded, then disappeared inside. He stayed in there longer than Nathaniel would have expected. Maybe the man was finishing his morning meal? Nathaniel really should have waited another half hour at least before coming.

Finally the door opened again and Reuben strode out. Behind him came another man, the same older fellow from the other day. Hadn't he introduced himself as Grant? Another body stepped through the opening—the younger woman.

Nathaniel's mouth dried up at the sight of her.

Reuben motioned to the man. "This is Simeon Grant and his daughter, Miss Hannah Grant. Is it all right if they ride along? If you want to move any of the stock today, they can help."

The woman wanted to talk animals with the neighbors? And help drive said animals back? Could she even do that in a sidesaddle? He scrambled for an appropriate response. "Oh, um…sure." He should have settled for a nod. His mind and mouth were clearly disconnected.

She gave him a half-smile that didn't meet her eyes, nothing like the angelic look from when he'd seen her on the porch. Maybe this was best. If he'd be spending a good part of the day in her company, he'd better steel himself against her charms.

He followed the group toward the barn and fed hay to the animals as Reuben directed while the others saddled their horses. Miss Grant managed her own animal, without even an offer of help from her father. Interesting.

Before long, they were on the trail. He started off trying to make small talk with Reuben and Mr. Grant, something he wasn't very good at. But neither seemed especially talkative. Actually, it seemed like Grant might have conversed easily, but every time the man spoke, his glance slid to Reuben as though he wasn't sure how much he should say.

What exactly was going on with those two? Nathaniel almost turned his conversation to Miss Grant. She didn't ride sidesaddle as he'd expected, but sat astride as though she'd spent every day of her life on horseback. Focusing his attentions on her would simply get him into trouble with himself. Best he relax into the silence and enjoy the ride.

O'Hennessey turned out to be a pleasant fellow. The lines on his face proved he was getting up there in age, but he still moved like a man accustomed to hard work. Lord willing, Nathaniel would be that capable when he'd doubled his twenty-five years.

They rode down the mountain to give Nathaniel a chance to take a look at the stock. O'Hennessey said he was happy to part with a dozen or so cattle. As long as the animals seemed healthy and young enough to keep calving, Nathaniel would probably take them all. Wasn't a cow a cow? Horses, though, were another animal altogether.

He knew exactly what qualities he wanted in the horses he raised. Strong animals with hardy hooves, horses capable of riding long distances over rough terrain. Long-legged and muscled, too, so they could carry cavalry troopers of all shapes and sizes.

The animals he and his mother had raised for the cavalry back in Virginia had always contained a strong portion of Thoroughbred, for both height and speed. But when he came west, he noticed the horses weren't quite as tall but possessed a wiry endurance that served him and the other troopers well on many campaigns.

Sergeant Glover said many of them were native to this land, sometimes Indian ponies. He'd love to find some of these animals and cross them with the Thoroughbred stock he knew and loved. The horses that resulted would be perfectly suited for cavalry life, and would bring him a pretty penny, no doubt.

The sound of lowing cattle drifted to them before they rounded the trees to reveal a clearing of thick grass. A herd of at least fifty gleaming animals grazed in the area, their coloring a diverse collection of brown, black, or white. At least a third of them were calves, and most of the youngsters were a rich reddish brown. A reflection of the bull, no doubt.

O'Hennessey was doing well for himself.

They all reined to a stop, and Nathaniel couldn't help but glance sideways at Miss Grant. Loose tendrils of her pretty auburn hair played around her face, and her skin wore a healthy glow from the sun and the ride.

In truth, she was captivating, and he was quickly becoming much more interested in her than livestock. He needed to keep his wits about him.

"If there are any bull calves or yearlings you wanna raise to sire your herd, you're welcome to any of them." O'Hennessey's gravelly voice broke through his thoughts, pulling his focus back to the animals, where it ought to be. "If you wanna pick through the females and decide on ten or twelve, I'll let ya know the price for 'em all."

Nathaniel nodded, then glanced at Reuben. Did he have good experience knowing which be the healthiest and most likely to produce strong calves? Simeon Grant looked as if he may have more knowledge than any of them. Something about the man bespoke competence.

The older man met his gaze, and the corners of his mouth tipped in an easy smile. "These seem a bit like my herd. Shall we have a closer look?"

Hannah watched as Mr. Peak, Reuben, and her father rode around the outskirts of the cattle, pointing at some as the rumble of their voices sounded across the clearing. Mr. O'Hennessey had dismounted and was walking among the animals, rubbing heads and murmuring to them. The man who drew her gaze like a compass to true north was Mr. Peak.

He looked younger than Reuben by three or four years, and his manner was so engaging, as if he had a zeal for life that wouldn't be held down. Maybe that was why he was willing to take on so much, what with starting a ranch in these mountains. Storing up enough hay to feed even a dozen cattle and a few horses would take one man all summer. Surely he planned to hire help.

Did he have a wife somewhere? The thought sent an ache through her chest. Wouldn't he have said something if he had? At least to Reuben.

Her new brother had only said the man served in the cavalry for four years—a fact which didn't stand in his favor if he was anything like the Mounted Police stationed at the forts around their ranch. Those men could be hard—even brutal at times—in their enforcement of the trading laws and efforts to keep the natives quelled.

Was Mr. Peak like that too? He seemed so amiable, yet every man possessed a temper. Did he know how to keep his in check?

The man in question turned his attention to Mr. O'Hennessey, and the two held an animated conversation as they pointed to several cattle. Probably haggling over pricing.

At last, they both nodded, and the men set to work cutting cattle from the herd. It was time she step in and lend a hand.

When she rode near them, Pa pointed out a red heifer, probably no more than two years old. "Can you cull that one?"

She nodded and set to work, guiding her gelding around the animal. They'd performed this task so many times with Pa's stock, it wasn't hard for either of them to read the cow's mind.

This one balked at leaving her companions, but they soon had her trotting toward the group of animals collecting to the side. O'Hennessey stood guard on his horse to keep the cluster from spreading back into the herd.

Within a few minutes, they had twelve cows and a young bull in the group. She guided her horse toward Pa and Reuben while Mr. Peak settled up with their host.

Before long, they said farewell to Mr. O'Hennessey and set off with the small herd toward Mr. Peak's ranch.

"You have a pasture in mind to take them to?" Reuben glanced at Mr. Peak.

His gaze wandered into the distance. "The grassy area nearest my cabin is partway down the mountain I live on. I'm not sure of any shortcuts from here."

Reuben nodded. "I know the way."

As they traveled, they fell into a rhythm with Papa and Reuben riding lead on either side of the herd. She and Mr. Peak brought up the rear, spread out enough to keep any cattle from lagging behind.

The going was slow through the woods, but finally a beam of bright sunlight shone through the trees ahead.

As her father and Reuben emerged from the woods onto what looked like a rocky mountainside, one of the cows darted to the left, heading toward the sunshine farther up the mountain.

She kicked her gelding forward, charging up to cut off the animal's escape. The cow was quick, though, weaving through the trees faster than her horse could. She was just gaining the upper hand when they broke through the edge of the tree line.

Boulders dotted the mountainside, and her horse had to skirt them while keeping a fast clip to stay abreast of the cow, who wouldn't be steered down the mountain. Not yet anyway.

The cow was running so fast when she finally forced it to veer down toward the game trail, that the runaway was well in front of the rest of the animals.

At last, she had the cow on the trail, and she halted her gelding a little ways above the frightened bovine so it would stay put and wait for the rest of the herd to catch up. Both she and her horse were breathing hard, and the warm sun was already making beads of sweat run down her back.

A movement to the right snagged her attention. On a large boulder just beside the trail, something shifted. Her chest seized as the image clarified in her mind.

A snake.

The creature was curled in a thick circle with its head raised in a striking position. The other end stood up in the air, and the rattles marking the last section of tail were impossible to miss.

She reached for her rifle, even as she flicked a glance to see what would be in striking range for the reptile.

Reuben.

Her new brother was riding at the front of the herd, his focus on the cow on the trail ahead. He couldn't see the snake that was only half a horse-length away from him, and with the clatter of hooves on the rocky ground, he wouldn't hear the rattle that was surely sounding as the snake shook its thick tail.

She raised her hands to her mouth to scream a warning. "Reuben, turn back!"

But even as she cried out, a knife whizzed through the air, slicing through the snake's neck.

Reuben must have heard the sound, for he jerked his horse backward, craning to see up on the boulder.

The snake's body tumbled forward, falling off the rock and out of her sight.

"Are you hurt?" Her father's voice held an edge of panic as he turned to face his son.

Reuben held his reins tight, his focus on the trail in front of him, probably watching to see if the snake still lived. "I'm not."

At last, he raised his focus and turned to their father, who'd pulled his horse to a stop just behind Reuben's mare. "That was quick thinking. I hadn't even seen it."

Her father let out a long breath, his shoulders sinking with the exhale. "My only thought was that I couldn't stand to lose you again."

A long look passed between the two men, a look that raised a knot of emotion to clog Hannah's throat.

If no other good came of this journey, the love shimmering in her father's eyes as he looked upon his firstborn made every long hour in the saddle worth it.

She'd had the look turned on her many a time and knew well the swell of responding love it could raise. She could only hope she'd never give cause for that expression to be denied her. After all, she wasn't connected by blood to the man she loved so dearly.

He'd chosen to take her as his own, a choice she worked hard to keep him from regretting.

Chapter Five

They say forgiveness is more blessed to the giver than the receiver. But this gift is the most blessed of all.

~ Simeon

With the cattle assembled in a line to maneuver the terrain, they set off again.

It didn't escape Hannah's notice that her father now rode in the lead. A shift she was certain was his own doing. And she didn't blame him. Her father's care for his own ran deep in his soul, spreading to every action.

Mr. Peak glanced over at her, his gaze dipping down to her horse. "That's a nice gelding you have. Seemed like he could almost read the cows' minds as you were cutting them from the herd, then again when that cow took off up the mountain."

She patted Sterling's neck. "It's taken years to get that good, but he's a smart fellow." It was impossible to keep the man's words from warming her. She and Sterling had worked hard to develop their skills and the bond that connected them.

He tipped his head, and this time his gaze was focused on her. "Your family have a ranch around here?"

"In Canada, not far above the border. We live in a little valley surrounded by mountains on all sides." One corner of her mouth tugged. "Surrounded by mountains…and lots of family."

His brows rose. "Really?"

"Aunts, uncles, and cousins in every direction. Even though we're three days' ride from the nearest fort, none of us ever wanted for playmates growing up."

His eyes danced, but something else shone in them, too. Longing?

Maybe she should turn the questions on him. "What of you, Mr. Peak? From where do you hail?"

The merriment left his gaze. "From Virginia. And we lived a half hour's ride from town, but I didn't have nearly as much family around as you. Only my mother and grandmother for most of my life."

Now it was her turn to tip her head. "No neighbors to play with?"

He shrugged. "There was too much to do on the farm, it didn't leave time for playing."

"What kind of farm?" A picture was beginning to form of this man, but she still had holes to fill.

"Horses. We raised them for the cavalry mostly."

The cavalry again. He must be a staunch supporter if that group of soldiers had been part of his life from his earliest days.

She studied him out of the corner of her eye. Did she dare ask about his time serving in active duty? She'd like to know what sort of man he was, but... Maybe she should leave well enough alone.

She'd wanted to see new places and meet new people on this journey. Maybe even find a husband now that she'd left the little valley that had been her life for the past twenty-four years.

But she'd do best not to fall headlong for the first man she met. Especially when she still hadn't worked out the details of his character.

For now, she'd hold her tongue and try not to stare at his handsome face.

Ax in hand, Reuben strode toward the elm lying in wait in the woods, but a lone figure caught his attention.

Simeon stood in the corner of the clearing near where Pa was buried. The man's head dipped low, his hands clasped in front of him. A lonely figure.

And one Reuben could no longer avoid.

After reading the letters in his Pa's own hand, notes that contained updates and tales from Reuben's younger years, he could no longer refute what this man claimed.

Simeon Grant had sired him.

Then given him and his sister away for others to raise. The shock was slowly giving way to a kind of bitterness. An emotion he didn't want to feel. After all, he'd loved his parents. This had been a good life.

But why would a father give away his children? He could well imagine the grief he must have been under, losing his wife so suddenly. If Cathleen were snatched away from Reuben, he may well lose his mind. But he would want to cling to whatever of hers she left behind.

Especially their children.

Yet, what if clutching tight to those babes meant their likely death? The way Simeon had explained it, he'd been facing winter in the mountain country with no shelter. Could they have survived in those conditions? Tiny babes born before their time?

It was an impossible question.

But as he walked toward the man, he tried to imagine himself in his shoes. He'd want to give his children the best life he could, even if it meant never seeing them again.

And he would likely regret that choice for years to come. He would pray for the chance—just one opportunity to see them. To see his son grown to manhood. To know that boy-turned-man had enjoyed a good life. Loving parents.

The least Reuben could do was assure him of that.

He stopped beside the man, a few strides separating them as they stared at the same plot of land. Not Pa's grave, but little Nora's.

Of course.

Long silence stretched between them. Was Simeon lost in memories? Struggling through fresh grief?

His words finally gave the answer. "I thought I was doing the right thing." His voice rasped as if he'd dragged it over sharp stones. "The best thing for you both. I never knew how much I would regret leaving you. How much I would miss you."

A burn crept up Reuben's throat. He could imagine that feeling. And he could no longer find fault with Simeon's choice. This man who'd given them life really had thought he was doing the best for him and Nora.

And maybe his choice had been right.

Reuben cleared the lump from his throat. "We— I...had a fine life. Mum and Pa were good to me. I understand how hard that choice must have been for you. I don't know what our lives would have looked like if you'd decided the other way, but *what if's* don't matter at the end of the day. You made the choice you felt was right, and God worked good from it." He'd not meant to say so much. He wasn't even sure where the words came from. But as the silence settled again, he realized he'd meant every bit.

At last, Simeon turned and looked straight at him, his gaze strong and steady. "I want you to know how proud I am of you. I never dreamed—" His voice broke and his throat worked. "I never let myself hope you would turn out so well. Such a fine man." His gaze slipped to the house. "A wife who loves you." Simeon turned back to him, and this time his eyes glistened. "God heard every one of my prayers, and you're more than I hoped to dream."

Tears stung Reuben's own eyes, and he had to blink to hold them back. His father—the man who gave him life—

was proud of him. He couldn't even remember a time Pa had said that. Maybe he had, it was hard to recall just now.

All the response he could manage was a nod and a single word. "Thanks."

Simeon seemed to understand his emotion, for he reached a hand to clasp Reuben's shoulder. "Well, then. Are you headed back to work on the elm?"

Reuben nodded. "Thought I'd get the branches chopped for firewood." A thought slipped in, not one he'd planned to offer. "There's an old ax in the barn. The blade needs sharpened, but you're welcome to it if you want to help."

Simeon's response was slower in coming than he expected, and when Reuben raised his gaze to his father, he caught that glimmer in his eyes again. His Adam's apple bobbed. "I'd like that."

Nathaniel slid down from his mare when he reached his barn, pulling the door wide so he and the animal could both get out of the rain. Three days since Reuben and his guests had helped drive Nathaniel's new cattle to his pastures, and it had rained two of them. He wasn't getting much done at this rate.

But after working in the downpour all morning, he was more than ready to dry out and heat himself some warm grub. He could almost taste the leftover beans from what he'd cooked the night before.

The barn's interior was dark with no lanterns lit, and the drum of rain outside drowned out most of the normal sounds. He'd always loved the noise of drops pelting the roof, but he was too wet to enjoy it just now. Maybe once he was in the house, in dry clothes and with his belly full.

He let Raven stand in the aisle while he stripped the saddle and dried the leather. He didn't have hay cut yet, so he'd been staking the horse out to graze each night. That wouldn't do right now with all this rain. Surely Raven would prefer a dry stall for the moment, then they could find a grassy area later.

He led the horse to the enclosure on the end—the only one that didn't have a leak in the ceiling overhead. Raven balked at the entrance. "Come on, girl. I know it's dark in there, but it's also dry."

Nathaniel stepped into the stall first, scanning the area to make sure it was as he'd left it. Darkness hugged the corners, but all seemed as before. He turned his focus back to the horse and tugged the reins to pull her in. Raven's ears stood at alert, her nostrils breathing deeply as she stepped inside. Something wasn't right with the horse's behavior. Simple darkness shouldn't worry her this much.

Nathaniel's hand went to the knife at his hip as he peered into the darkness. First one corner, then the next. His nerves eased a little each time he saw through the shadows to confirm all was well. He raised his gaze to check the rafters as he moved around Raven to see the other two corners.

Nothing.

Then a shadow shifted behind the stall door.

He tensed, jerking his hunting knife from its sheath. "Who's there?" He strained to see into the darkness and finally made out a shapeless form. A blanket thrown over something.

A whimper sounded from the object. Almost like that of a…puppy?

"Who's there?" He kept his voice gruff as he inched forward. Just in case this was a ploy to catch him off guard. But by who? He had no enemies, not unless you counted the hundreds of Indians he'd helped confine to the reservations. The men he'd fought, then women and children he'd restrained.

He locked his jaw against the memories. He had to keep his wits about him.

Whatever was buried under that cloth didn't answer, but the fabric shifted.

Could an animal be under there? How could a creature drag that blanket in here and hide underneath?

He was close enough now to reach out and jerk the cloth away. If only he had his gun. If an Indian hid under that shroud with a rifle pointed at him, his knife would be little defense.

But a grown Indian couldn't be that small, could he? Whatever was there didn't come up higher than Nathaniel's knee.

Inhaling a strengthening breath, he raised his knife in a striking position. Then he reached out, grabbed the cloth, and jerked it away with a hard pull.

A yelp sounded, and Nathaniel struggled to make sense of what he was seeing. A mass of black hair shielded a tiny person. A child? The whites of large, fear-filled eyes stared back at him.

If only he had a lantern. "Who are you?" He softened his voice this time, still trying to see the details of the youngster. It looked like a girl, both from the shape of the face and the long, tangled hair. But he could be wrong on that.

The sharp cheekbones, dark eyes, and black hair proclaimed her to be an Indian, and she couldn't be more than four or five. Maybe six.

He dropped to his knees beside her. He wanted to ease her fright, but perhaps it was not a good choice to make himself so vulnerable in case her guardian crept into the stall behind him.

He shifted around to the side so he could see the doorway out of the corner of his eye. The child pulled back as he moved, fear emanating from her in waves.

"I'm not going to hurt you. Where did you come from?" *And how did you get in my barn?* Someone must have brought her, then left her there—maybe because of the rain—and would return for her soon.

He needed his rifle. And the child probably needed food and a dry blanket. He reached out to see how wet her covering was.

She shrank back even farther, and then her face contorted as she gave a cry of pain.

"Are you hurt?" He scanned her body but couldn't see anything except a mass of dirty buckskins. In truth, the child was a muddy mess.

"I'm going to get something for you to eat. Stay here. Do you understand?" She hadn't spoken yet, and likely didn't know a word he said. But he needed a lantern so he could determine what was wrong with her. And she was likely in desperate need of food and a warm blanket. Maybe those gifts would help her see he wanted to help.

Easing away, he stood and reached for Raven's reins as he spoke to the horse. "Let's move you to a different stall so she doesn't get stepped on." Perhaps they'd find the girl's guardian in the next pen over. His mouth twitched at his mind's attempt at humor.

No Indians presented themselves in the stall corners, and he quickly settled Raven, then slipped out of the barn and jogged through the rain to the cabin. He scanned trees around the clearing as he ran, but nothing seemed unusual.

Was an Indian watching him, even now? His neck crawled at the thought.

Inside, he grabbed a chunk of cornbread and scooped a bowl of beans. The food was cold, but would fill her belly. He scooped a cup of water, too. After lighting a lantern, he pulled a wool blanket from his sleeping pallet and loaded up the food, then headed back out in the rain.

The barn felt eerie as he stepped inside, but that was likely his imagination. Just in case, he shone the lantern in

59

each of the stalls to make sure he didn't have other unknown guests. He half-expected the girl to be gone now that she'd been discovered, but she still sat where he left her.

Such a tiny waif with her blanket wrapped around her. Only her face showed through tendrils of stringy hair.

He dropped to his knees beside her again and laid out the things he'd brought. "Here's some food for you." He pointed toward the beans, then made a motion as though bringing some to his mouth. "And a blanket. Let's get you warm."

Opening up the covering, he reached to wrap it around the girl's shoulders. Again, she shrank back, but he kept on with his action, and she allowed him to wrap his blanket over her own. It would be better to remove the wet covering, but this would have to do for now. She didn't look like she'd allow him to take it.

Next, he picked up the bowl and placed it in front of her, taking the spoon and lifting it up with a bite of beans like he was going to feed her. He stopped halfway to her mouth, then set the spoon down and motioned for her to do it. "Eat."

Her wary gaze dipped from his face to the food, then rose to his face again. She reached for the bowl, never moving her focus from him. When she took the first bite, he let out a tense breath. Now surely she'd eat the rest.

He kept his senses on alert for sounds in the barn around them as she ate, and when she'd scarfed down half the beans, he pushed the cornbread and water closer to her.

This was a lot of food for such a little thing, but she looked hungry enough to swallow it whole.

While she ate, he scanned the rest of her body. She was curled up in a ball, but something didn't look right with her legs. One muddy moccasin peeked out from beneath the blanket, but the angle seemed odd. He needed to know if she was hurt or sick so he could help her. But it would take some coaxing to get her to reveal any injuries.

When she'd finally eaten the last morsel and drained the cup, he pulled the dishes away from her. She wrapped the blankets tighter around herself, tucking into a ball. Pain slipped over her features with the movement, but she dipped her face into the shadows so quickly he caught only a glimpse. The moccasin peeking from the blanket never moved. Could she have a broken leg? It seemed like she'd be in tears if that were the case.

He motioned to his chest. "I'm Nathaniel." His name was such a mouthful for this sprite, he switched to the shortened version. "Nate."

Then he pointed to her and formed a question with his face.

She stared at him with a blank expression. Did she understand at all? Maybe she was too young.

He tried again, touching his chest as he spoke. "Nate."

This time, when he pointed to her, she hesitated only a minute before speaking in a tiny voice. "Itu." At least, that's what it sounded like. The word came out barely louder than a breath.

"Itu?" He repeated the sound as closely as he could.

She gave a single nod.

All right then. They were making progress.

He inched backward so he could work his leg out from under him. Patting his calf, he said, "Leg." Then he pointed to her leg. Would she understand and pull the blanket away?

Hesitation touched her features. He tapped his leg again and said the word, then motioned to hers. He was pretty sure she understood, but whether she would comply was another matter altogether.

Her lips formed a tight line, and something like fear slipped through her eyes. Then slowly, she eased the blanket away from her leg.

He was careful not to shift, not to do anything that would frighten her. As the covering pulled away, it revealed a moccasin that covered the child's lower leg. Just above the ankle was a red gash that split the leather in a jagged tear.

But the thing that stole Nathaniel's breath was the gruesome, unnatural angle of her foot.

Chapter Six

This may well be my greatest shock of all.

~ Nathaniel

As Nathaniel peered closer at the child's leg, he had to swallow down the bile that threatened to rise. What had caused that injury? An animal attack? A steel trap? What did her leg look like underneath the moccasin? That foot had to be broken.

The shoe needed to be removed, but only the top part could be unlaced. If the bone was severed, the lower leather would have to be cut off. Even if he accomplished that, he'd never set a broken bone before. He had a few salves with his supplies, but probably not anything as strong as she'd need if her wound was festering.

In short, he needed help, someone with more knowledge and medicine than he possessed.

Reuben was his closest neighbor. Maybe someone there could either help or ride for a doctor.

Should he try to take Itu there? If her leg was broken, moving her on horseback would be excruciating. And if her guardian returned and found her missing, what would he or she do? Reuben's cabin was almost an hour's ride away. If he left her here, then when he returned, the girl might be gone.

He hated to inconvenience his neighbors, but he couldn't in good conscience move this child in her condition. It would be helpful if he could get a look at the wound before he left, though. That way he'd be better able to determine the extent of the help needed.

"Itu." He motioned to the leather covering her leg. "I need to cut your moccasin off."

Her wide eyes searched his, but she didn't pull away as his hand neared. He reached closer and touched the buckskin at the top. He could almost feel her body tense, but she didn't flinch as he untied the lacing and began to work the cords loose. His fingers were so big and clumsy, taking twice as long as they should have to pull the ties free.

The leather gradually separated, revealing puffy, bluish skin. The farther down he went, the deeper the bruising. Whatever had wounded her had done a great deal of damage.

The laces ended before he reached the gash in the leather, and her leg was so swollen, he wasn't able to look down into the shoe to see more. He'd have to cut the rest off, which would require pulling out his knife and frightening the poor girl even more.

He chanced a look up at her. Terror and pain mingled in her wide gaze, and the whites of her eyes had turned red from unshed tears. She was a remarkably brave child to be in this condition—alone—and not falling into hysteria.

Another glance at the leg convinced him not to cut the moccasin off just yet. Maybe the leather would keep the swelling down and hold the foot in place until he returned with someone who could tend the injuries correctly.

He pulled the blanket back over the wound and looked into Itu's eyes. "I'm going to get someone who can help you. A healer. Stay here until I return."

She stared at him, a glimmer of trust in her gaze. At least, he hoped that was trust.

"Stay here." He held out a hand, palm toward her like he was training a dog to the command. She didn't make any sign she understood, but he'd have to go in the hope she'd still be here when he returned.

He pulled Raven back out of the stall and saddled him with the quick precision he'd learned from all his training in the cavalry. This was one good thing that had come of those four years.

The rain hadn't lessened when he stepped outside. He mounted and pushed the horse into as fast a trot as he dared over the slick ground. It seemed to take hours to reach the Scotts' place, but finally he spotted the break in the trees that signaled the trail to their clearing.

At the porch, he jumped from the saddle, hearing the sound of a dog barking inside. The door swung open as he jogged up the steps. Finally under the shelter of the porch roof, he paused to catch his breath.

"Come in, Peak. What's wrong?" Reuben stepped aside to allow him access, but Nathaniel didn't move forward. There wasn't time for chit-chat, and he had no wish to soil their floor with his muddy boots and dripping clothes.

He shook his head. "I'm in need of a doctor." His breath still came in jagged gasps, and he paused to suck in a deep draft of air.

"What's wrong? Are you sick?" Reuben's wife joined him in the doorway, worry clouding her features.

Again he shook his head. "A girl. Found her in my barn. Her leg is swollen, looks like it might be broken." Now his breath was coming easier. "She's young, maybe five years old. I didn't take her moccasin off all the way, so I'm not sure if it's an animal bite or if she stepped in a trap. She needs someone who can set the bone and give her something for pain and healing."

Mrs. Scott disappeared from the doorway, and Reuben's face had turned grim. He reached for his coat from a peg on the wall. "We'll come do what we can. Cathleen was a nurse once. If she can't help, I'll go for one of the doctors." He spun away, leaving Nathaniel standing in front of the open doorway.

From the voices he could distinguish, Mr. Grant was also inside, and the two men exchanged quiet conversation. Women's tones sounded from the room, and he couldn't miss the soft cadence of Miss Grant's voice.

In less than a minute, that same woman appeared in the doorway, coat on and a man's hat atop her head. "I'm going to saddle the horses."

He stepped aside to let her through but couldn't seem to take his eyes from the unlikely combination of her pretty face under what must have been her father's worn felt hat.

She didn't give him a second look as she marched off the porch into the rain. He could certainly help ready the animals.

After hurrying to untie Raven, he jogged with the horse to catch up to her, sloshing in mud as they went. She had a long stride and didn't stop to wait for him. In the barn, she pointed to the third stall down. "You can saddle those last two for Reuben and Cathleen. I'll get these others."

She gave the command easily, all efficiency as she set to work. Apparently, there would be quite a group going to tend little Itu.

He tied Raven and dove into his task, making quick work of readying the animals. Once again, he was grateful for the quick efficiency he'd learned in the cavalry. As he hoped, Miss Grant wasn't quite finished with the two she'd taken on, and he stepped in to take over with her father's horse.

They worked together in silence, and he could feel the tension radiating from her. When she led her gelding to meet him in the barn aisle, her pretty face looked troubled. "Was there any sign of how the girl came into your barn? Who would have left her there so injured?"

His chest squeezed as that terrified little face flashed through his mind. "I'm sure they'll be back for her. I just hope we can tend her leg before they take her." A renewed urgency pressed through him.

She nodded and reached for the reins of her father's horse. "Let's go."

Within minutes, they were mounted and formed a formidable party—Reuben, his wife, Mr. Grant, Miss Grant, and of course, Nathaniel. He couldn't help feeling he was back in the B Troop, heading out with a contingent of cavalry.

He could only hope they didn't frighten Itu so much they made her situation worse.

When they reached the clearing where his cabin lay, they reined down to a walk. Thankfully, the downpour had slowed to a misty drizzle. He scanned the area for signs of Indians, but all seemed quiet.

He halted his horse outside the barn and slid to the ground. "She's in the last stall, but I think if we all barge in there, we're going to scare her. I'll go in first just to make sure she hasn't been stolen away."

Reuben slipped from his own horse. "I'll come too, just in case her people are in there. I know some Crow."

"Good. Maybe you can tell her we only want to help." He reached for his knife as he pulled open the barn door. He'd left the lantern in the stall with Itu, and light still shone from that corner.

No Indians jumped out at them, but he and Reuben checked each stall just in case. All was quiet as they advanced. Not even a peep from the little girl he prayed was still where he'd left her.

"Itu?" He spoke her name as they approached her hiding place. "I've brought someone to help you."

No tiny voice answered.

He peered over the stall door and breathed out his relief. The tiny figure huddled under the blanket he'd brought her. "I'm glad you're still here." He stepped inside with Reuben on his heels, then dropped to his knees in front of her.

"This is my friend, Reuben." He motioned to the man kneeling beside him.

Reuben spoke a string of sounds in what must be Crow.

The girl's eyes widened. She answered in the same kind of high-low cadence. Reuben spoke again, and the girl's response sounded like the same answer she'd given before. Maybe Nathaniel's ear wasn't attuned to the sounds the way it should be.

Reuben responded again, but his brow wrinkled with his words. Was it bad news then?

The girl answered, her reply shorter this time.

Nathaniel could wait no longer. "What did she say?"

Reuben turned to him. "She's not Crow. I think she's speaking the language of the Hidatsa, but I've never seen them this far west. The two tongues are similar, so I might be able to communicate with her some."

"Can you tell her we have other people who've come to help her?" He couldn't leave the others out in the weather any longer. "I'm going to bring them in." He offered a smile to Itu, then eased back out of the stall.

He filled the others in as they led the animals inside.

"I'll tie the horses." Miss Grant reached for the reins from her father and Mrs. Scott.

Nathaniel couldn't leave her to tend five animals by herself, but he wanted to be there to introduce Itu to these new strangers. For some reason, he felt a fierce need to protect the child from anything that might cause more stress to a girl who must already be terrified and in a great deal of pain.

He and Miss Grant quickly secured the horses, and she followed him toward the back stall.

Reuben was speaking to the child in the same melodic language he'd used before, but her eyes had grown impossibly round as she stared at all the adults crowding around her.

Her gaze locked on Nathaniel as he entered, and he moved around to the wall so he could be near and reach a calming hand to her. She seemed almost relieved when he laid his palm on her blanketed shoulder.

"These are friends." He motioned to the others and tried to offer a smile. "Help."

She still kept her solemn gaze on him as though he held the answers to all her trouble. *Help me, Lord.*

He pointed to her leg, covered again by the blankets. "Leg." He touched the covering.

Reuben spoke something in Crow, and her gaze darted to him. The man must be close to fluent. Nathaniel would have to ask him sometime how he'd learned.

70

Itu cautiously eased the blankets aside from her leg as her focus returned to Nathaniel's face. He tried to give her an encouraging smile and nod.

When her moccasin finally showed, Nathaniel reached forward and separated the leather that he'd already untied, revealing the grossly swollen and bruised flesh. "I haven't cut the rest of the moccasin off to see whether the bone is broken where the leather is torn here, but I'm pretty certain it is." He kept his tone soft as he pointed to the rip just above her ankle.

"That's definitely from a trap. Wolf or small animal, probably. If it was a bear trap, she'd still be screaming from the pain." Reuben's voice was low, but held a certainty that bespoke experience. He reached for the knife at his belt as he spoke another slew of Crow.

Itu's eyes flashed terror when she saw the blade, and she shrank back against the barn wall.

"It's all right." Nathaniel added a little more certainty to the hand resting on her shoulder. But truly, if he were a tiny girl hurt and alone, with adults staring at her and a man brandishing a hunting knife near her injured leg, he'd be panicking, too. She needed a mother to hold and soothe her. How could anyone have left her here in this condition?

He raised his gaze to Mrs. Scott, Reuben's wife. She was the nurse, right? Surely she knew how to calm a fearful child. But she was murmuring with Simeon Grant, both of them eyeing the girl's leg. Probably planning which medical approach would be best.

His focus wandered to Miss Grant. Her eyes held a depth of sadness as she watched Itu, but she seemed to feel him looking at her. She met his gaze, and maybe he showed his worry in his eyes, for her chin bobbed in a tiny nod. She quietly moved around beside him.

Nathaniel shifted back to allow her room next to the girl.

Itu stared at Miss Grant with those luminous eyes, and the woman leaned low so she was face to face with the girl. She raised a hand to stroke the dark stringy hair from Itu's cheeks, and Nathaniel could almost feel the gentleness in the caress.

The child's eyes softened a little, and Miss Grant held the pose for a long moment. Then she straightened and worked herself against the wall beside Itu, wrapping her arms around the girl. She continued stroking her hair and began humming a soft melody, as though the rest of them weren't there.

Miss Grant's gaze shifted to Nathaniel, and her eyes formed a sad smile as she lay her head against the little girl's. Her humming never ceased, and he could feel the way it relaxed even his own muscles.

Little by little, Itu snuggled into her. She didn't even seem to notice when Reuben moved the knife closer and cut a slit down the leather of her moccasin. The buckskin separated to reveal more swollen, purple skin and an angry gash in the flesh. No bone protruded through the skin—a good thing. But the unusual twist of the foot below the ankle had to mean a break.

A glance at the other's faces, with the grim pinch of Reuben's mouth and the deepening lines across Mr. Grant's brow, proved they were just as concerned about the injury.

Chapter Seven

How is it the pain of this child can so fully infect my own heart?

~ Hannah

Nathaniel watched as Mr. Grant turned to Reuben's wife. "I've set breaks like that before, but only because we don't have a doctor near where we live. Do you think it's realistic to wait for one of your doctor brothers to come secure the limb? How far away did you say they live?"

"In Butte," Mrs. Scott said. "It's about a five-hour ride each direction. I'm sure one of them would come if someone went for them. It would be tomorrow before they could get here, though."

"I can ride to Butte." Reuben glanced at the leg again, then back to his wife. "I think we should wrap some kind of splint around it until then."

"I have some herbals that will help with pain and swelling." Mr. Grant again.

"Once her leg is secure, we should move her to the house." Mrs. Scott looked at Nathaniel. "If that's all right."

His mind called up an image of his sparse, rickety cabin. "The place isn't much, but it'll be better than here." He didn't even have a wood floor laid yet.

Mr. Grant nodded as he rose. "All right then. I'll get the medicines I brought and look for wood to splint the leg until the doctor can come."

Reuben and his wife left the stall with the older man. The place felt almost empty with only Nathaniel, Miss Grant, and little Itu, and when he turned his focus back to them, the sight of the little girl's relaxed expression as Miss Grant cradled and hummed to her sent a warmth through his chest.

Whether she was cutting cattle from a herd or soothing frightened children, this woman knew exactly when to step in and take action. And she had a way about her that made you believe she'd make everything work out in the end.

He sat there watching them, soaking in the sight of Miss Grant's pretty face in the lamplight. The glow made her auburn hair take on a fiery gleam, the perfect representation of both her strength and beauty.

He'd do best not to linger there any longer. Rising to his knees, he let himself take in one last look. "I'm going to build a fire and ready a bed for her in the house. Is there anything else you need?"

Miss Grant met his gaze, her brown eyes serene, even with the flame flickering in their depths. "I'm sure she's hungry, but I can see to that once we get her inside."

He nodded. "I gave her a bowl of beans and cornbread, but that's been a few hours. I'll have more heating." He hoped she liked beans, cornbread, and roasted meat, because that was all he had to offer, and even some of those supplies were getting thin.

Soon he'd have to make time to ride down to Butte to restock.

Setting the little girl's leg was excruciating for all of them, and tears were running down both Hannah's cheeks and the child's by the time they were finished splinting the leg. Hannah could feel the pain trembling through the little body, and she longed to take the ache into herself.

Anything to lessen the torment.

At last, Papa eased away from the splint he'd wrapped. The lines across his face had thickened with the strain of the past half hour. "Let's get her inside and steep some willow tea. Reuben, do you want to carry her?" Her father was probably spent from his efforts thus far.

She almost volunteered to carry the waif herself. The child couldn't be heavier than her youngest cousins when she'd started toting them around, but Reuben's strength would help keep Itu's leg steady as he walked.

Reuben bent down in front of the girl and spoke in his Crow tongue to her, likely telling what they were about to do. Hannah could feel the tension heighten in the child, as she must have understood some of it.

Itu shook her head hard and clutched Hannah's arms, holding her tight.

Hannah dropped her face so she could murmur in the child's ear. "It's all right. We're not going far." She probably didn't understand a word, and Hannah almost didn't want to speak English to the girl, because it might make her feel even more alone. That's why she'd hummed earlier instead of speaking calming words.

Hannah switched to humming now. After a moment, she shifted her hands so she was holding the girl like a babe, one hand under her legs and the other around her back.

Itu still clung but didn't protest the movement. Maybe Hannah would need to carry her after all.

Carefully, she worked her legs up underneath her, then stood, grateful for Reuben's hand on her arm helping her rise with the load.

The girl was heavier than she'd looked.

Hannah thought briefly about handing the child over to Reuben now that she was standing, but Itu clung fiercely to her neck. Prying her away would be more traumatic than simply walking to the house.

A steady spattering of rain dripped from the sky as they stepped outside, and she ducked her head over the child's to keep her dry. It would take a long time in front of a warm fire to dry them, as damp as they both were already.

Cathleen held the cabin door open, and as Hannah stepped inside, she couldn't help but notice the way the door frame slanted a little. The wood looked as if it had seen more than one harsh winter. There was no porch, so she stepped on the flat rock meant for a stoop, then onto the transom. She expected her next step to land on the cabin's wood floor, but inside was another flat rock, then down to hard-packed ground. The place was dim with only the hearth fire and a lantern offering light.

Nathaniel met her partway into the room. "I've made a pallet by the fire." He motioned toward the bedding. "I used all the blankets I have, but they're probably still not very comfortable."

She moved to the bed and dropped to her knees, then lay Itu down on the blankets. The fire's warmth felt heavenly at her shoulder.

Cathleen was by her side, adjusting the girl's splinted leg and pulling out the blankets that had been wrapped around her before. She held up the darker one. "This is still wet. I'll lay it out to dry."

While Papa and the others brewed herbal tea and scooped out food, Hannah stayed with Itu, stroking her hair and soothing in any way she could. When Cathleen handed her a bowl of beans, she helped the girl eat. Itu could feed herself, but she seemed to prefer for Hannah to do it. She was surely exhausted from the pain and fear and whatever else she'd endured before Mr. Peak found her.

That thought spurred another, and she looked up at the men around her. "Do you think whoever brought her will worry when they don't find her in the barn? What will they do?" It might be too much to hope they'd come knock on the door and ask politely to see the child.

Reuben scrubbed a hand through his hair. "Watch and wait probably. Depending on whether it's a warrior or squaw." He looked pointedly at Mr. Peak. "Nathaniel, you need to stay on your guard. Keep your rifle with you at all times just in case. They'll probably be friendly if they don't think you've kidnapped the girl. Try to show you mean no harm."

Her brother glanced toward the door. "I need to head out if I'm going to make it to Butte tonight." He glanced at his wife. "I'll stop by our cabin and see how Emma's doing with Mum."

Cathleen pushed to her feet. "I'll ride back with you. I don't think there's much more I can do here. Simeon knows more than I do and has more supplies." She sent Papa a smile, and Hannah couldn't help a smile herself at the way her family seemed to be connecting with Reuben and his family.

"We should be going soon, too." Papa's voice settled over her like a weight. "I'll go through the herbs and explain what to give when."

He would leave this girl with Mr. Peak? She glanced at the man, whose face had paled. He still met her father's gaze, though, with a nod. Didn't he have work to do? His new cattle to tend? How could he do all that and care for an injured five-year-old, too?

She forced herself to speak up. "Papa, I'll stay and care for the girl. Mr. Peak won't be able to do his work and care for all of Itu's needs."

All eyes turned to her. Even Reuben stopped on his way to the door and looked back at her. She kept her chin raised. What she'd said was true, and a few shocked looks didn't change the fact.

79

Papa's gaze slid from her to Mr. Peak. What did he see there?

She didn't turn to look. This wasn't about Mr. Peak. It was about her desire to stay and help this sweet child feel better. There was so little for her to do back at Reuben's house, what with Mama and Cathleen in charge of everything.

Here, she was *needed*.

"I'll stay with you." Cathleen stepped forward. "We'll help her while Mr. Peak is working today, then return home just before dark."

Papa sighed. "No. Go home. I'll stay with Hannah and tend our charge." He sent a nod toward Cathleen and Reuben. "Let my wife know not to worry."

As the pair exited, Hannah tried not to let her frustration show. She was capable of staying with the girl on her own. And capable of dealing with this man in the process. He'd not given any cause for concern so far, but she had her rifle and could use it if the need arose. She turned back to Itu, stealing a glance at Mr. Peak as she did.

"Well." The man let out a breath. "I suppose I'll go settle our horses. I don't have hay cut yet, but at least I can unsaddle them. Is there anything you need while I'm out there?"

Papa nodded. "A few things, but I'll come out and lend a hand. Hannah, are you all right here alone?"

"Of course." At home, they'd not hesitate to send her into the mountains on her own to check a herd or out on a solo hunting trip. Why the overbearing concern now? Did her father distrust Mr. Peak?

Every time she began to feel more comfortable with the man, something new came up to raise her concerns.

Nathaniel almost missed the sound of approaching horses the next morning between blows from his ax. He lowered the tool and watched the trail into the clearing, his breath coming in hard gasps from the steady effort he'd been putting in. He really should be cutting hay, but he hadn't wanted to leave Itu that morning. So he'd set to work cutting slabs of wood to replace the rotten pieces on his door frame.

He hadn't planned to work on the house until the hay was cut and a corral fence built, but exposing the inadequacies of his home the day before had been embarrassing. Sure, he'd only been here about a month and his focus had been the animals, but he was used to being proud of his living space—whether it be their farm back in Virginia or his bunk at the fort. He'd never been slovenly, and the thought that his new neighbors might think him that way rubbed him wrong.

Besides, the doctor should come any time. Hopefully, that was him now.

Four figures emerged through the trees, two men and two women. He recognized the horses Reuben and his wife had ridden the day before, but it was the poised form of Miss Grant that drew his focus. He'd not let himself hope she would come back today. Mostly because he *shouldn't* hope it. He was doing a sorry job of keeping his interest at bay. If she would simply fade into the background instead of being so good at everything she set her mind to, she'd be easier to forget.

Wiping a sleeve across his forehead, he headed for the house. Itu had slept a lot that morning, which was good, for rest helped keep her mind off the pain. He'd go ahead and put some fresh water on to heat in case the doctor needed it. Come to think of it, he should probably rustle up some food for them all. A glance at the sun showed he'd missed the time for the midday meal. How had the day slipped away so far?

The girl opened her eyes when he stepped into the cabin.

He offered a smile. "You have visitors." Her eyes lit, and she spoke something he couldn't understand. Was she asking for Miss Grant? Itu had been so downcast when the woman and her father left the evening before.

He didn't blame the child. He'd rather see that pretty lady than his own ugly mug any day.

With the fire stoked and the pot of water moved to a warmer position, he strode back to let in their visitors. Miss Grant was the first face he saw as he pulled open the door, and his breath caught at the sheer prettiness of her features.

With her cheeks pinkened and her hair a bit windblown from the ride, seeing her this close made it hard to breathe.

Chapter Eight

Never in my wildest dreams did I think this would be my lot. Yet, I can't turn away.

~ Nathaniel

athaniel could feel the strength of Miss Grant's gaze as she searched his face.

"How is she?"

He forced himself to look away from the beauty in front of him, to step aside and motion toward the girl. "She's slept a lot today. I think she's eager to see you."

The woman strode across the room, her focus on nothing but the child. How nice it must have been to have all that loveliness centered on you.

Mrs. Scott stepped in next, followed by a man who must have been the doctor. The man extended his hand. "Doc Bryan Donaghue."

Nathaniel returned the clasp. "Nathaniel Peak. Thanks for coming so far."

As the doctor followed the women to Itu's bed, Nathaniel looked back out to see why Reuben hadn't come in, too. He held all four horses' reins and was walking toward the barn. "I'm going to tie them," he called over his shoulder.

Nathaniel should go help the man. Yet everything in him pulled him toward the group kneeling beside the little girl who had become his responsibility. So he called out to Reuben, "There's two open stalls. Feel free to use them."

Miss Grant had the girl wrapped in a hug by the time he made it over to them. The doctor was talking to the child while he examined the leg.

Itu didn't have the frightened look of the day before, not when she was holding tight to Miss Grant. Pain flashed through the child's eyes as the doctor unwrapped the cloth binding the splint.

Miss Grant looked up at Nathaniel as though she needed something, and he moved nearer.

"Do you have any willow tea made?" She spoke in a low voice that wouldn't distract the doctor.

He glanced toward the pot. "Not since midmorning when I gave her everything you left. I have water heating. Should I make some?"

She nodded. "It'll help with the pain."

That was right. Her father had mentioned that the night before, but he'd been so focused on exactly what to give when, he'd not stored the tidbit away in his mind. He should have thought ahead and had some ready for when the doctor arrived.

After setting the tea to steep, he turned back to watch the examination. He had to grit his teeth to keep his gorge down when the cloth covering fell away to reveal the bruised and swollen leg—at least twice the normal size from the knee down. The gash above the ankle was by far the worst, with the bright red tear split apart and oozing all manner of unsettling colors.

Even Doctor Donaghue's face held a grim line.

Miss Grant had taken up her humming and never stopped as she stroked the child's hair. She'd positioned herself in such a way that he didn't think Itu could see her injured leg. Was that intentional? Either way, he was thankful.

It seemed to take forever for the doctor to bandage the wound, then splint the leg. At last, he straightened and managed a smile for the girl. "You did so well, I have a sweet for you." He reached into his pocket and pulled out a peppermint, then held it out for the girl.

Itu only stared at the object. Miss Grant reached for the candy, then touched it to the girl's mouth with a smile and a nod. The little mouth opened, and the peppermint disappeared inside.

Gradually, a smile bloomed on the child's face as she stared at Miss Grant, lighting her eyes in a way that pressed hard on Nathaniel's chest. Then Itu looked to the doctor, and the smile turned shy.

He chuckled and patted the girl's arm. "Candy always helps."

Mrs. Scott had already packed the doctor's supplies back in his bag, a sure sign she'd worked with her brother before.

Doctor Donaghue looked from Nathaniel to Miss Grant. "Who will be the primary caretaker for her?"

"I will." They both spoke at once.

Nathaniel turned to Miss Grant. What did she mean by that? She couldn't be Itu's caretaker unless they moved the child to the Scotts' home.

Her face colored a little. "I mean, I'd like to be." She glanced at Nathaniel. "I guess we should talk about it."

"All right, then." The doctor pushed to his feet. "Perhaps you could both walk me to my horse."

Something about the doctor's manner, or maybe Miss Grant strolling just ahead of him, set Nathaniel's nerves on edge as the three of them stepped out the door.

The doctor made it halfway across the yard before he turned to face them both. His expression was almost as grim as it had been when he first saw the wound. "I have to say, that leg doesn't look good. There's been a great deal of damage to the muscle and tissue, and the wound is festering."

"How long ago do you think it happened?" Nathaniel was still trying to piece together where she'd come from and why someone would have left her alone so long in the barn. He'd seen no sign of a guardian returning for her. He'd been on the lookout for someone waiting in the woods, but there'd been no indication of anybody nearby.

Doctor Donaghue's forehead creased. "Several days, at least. Maybe four or five."

Four or five days with the injury left untreated. How much pain she must have been in.

"What should we do for her?" Miss Grant spoke up, always the doer.

"She needs to stay still for a while. At least a week. I'll try to come up and change the bandage by then. I'll have to unfasten the splint, and we can see how she's healing." He leveled a serious gaze on them both. "There's been so much damage, there's a chance the infection could spread or the tissues won't regrow."

The pressure in Nathaniel's chest rose up to his throat. "What does that mean?"

"She may lose the leg."

He could hear a gasp from Miss Grant, but his mind seemed to slow as he tried to process the words.

The doctor kept talking. "We'll make the decision when I come back as to whether she's healing or if we need to take the leg before things get worse. The sooner we act, the less she'll need to lose."

A hand gripped his arm, and without thinking, he laid his palm over Miss Grant's fingers. Poor Itu. How could she manage life with one leg missing?

He'd known men who lost limbs in the War Between the States, many of whom were bitter and sullen about their loss, becoming recluses and often simply fading away.

That couldn't happen to such a young child, one with her entire life ahead of her. She should be running and playing games with her friends—wherever they may be—not lying in his ramshackle cabin, threatened with the possible loss of a limb.

The doctor was speaking again, and Nathaniel forced his mind to focus on the man's words. "Keep giving her the herbs Mr. Grant left for her. Cathleen told me what they were, and he provided a good assortment. They'll help with the pain and healing from the inside."

He nodded. "Yes, sir."

The doctor heaved out a heavy breath. "I wish there was more I could do, but most of this will require waiting and praying." His gaze drifted to Miss Grant. "You can let my sister and her husband know I'll be readying the horses."

She nodded, but the gesture seemed stiff, almost wooden.

Nathaniel gave her hand a gentle squeeze, something to let her know they'd work their way through this. The action seemed to bring her alive, and her gaze darted to his as though she wasn't sure how she'd ended up with her hand on his arm.

She pulled away, then turned toward the house. "I'd better let Reuben and Cathleen know."

But she'd only gone a few steps before she stopped and spun back around. "Mr. Peak, I'd like to take Itu back with us to Reuben's house. I can care for her there. All of us can help. That way she won't interfere with your work."

Even though he'd half expected the request after her earlier comment, the idea of Itu leaving him slammed like a fist in his gut. She was his responsibility. Had been left in his barn. What if her people came back for her? They surely would. If they didn't speak English, he'd have no way of communicating where the girl was.

Misty M. Beller

And besides that, was it even safe to move her with the leg in such a precarious position? The doctor had said to keep her still. Surely that didn't involve an hour's ride to a different cabin.

"Do you agree?"

He had to answer her, but he hated to disappoint the hope lighting her features. Still, he shook his head. "I think she should stay here. I'll do what I need to for her care, and this is where her people will come to look for her. Besides, the doctor said not to move her."

Miss Grant's chin rose and her expression closed off. "He meant she shouldn't be allowed to get up and walk around. With us, I can keep her entertained, and we'll have plenty of food for her at all times."

Her words hit a spot already rubbed raw. Sure, he wasn't quite as stocked as he'd like to be, but Itu would never want for food as long as he could help it. "Miss Grant, I'm perfectly capable of feeding her as often as she wants to eat. Do you even have room for her over there? Seems like there's a mess of people in that one little cabin."

Her pretty brown eyes flared. "At least our cabin stands straight and doesn't let the rain blow in through the cracks."

A low blow but one he couldn't dodge. He worked to corral his anger, and he'd barely managed the feat when that very cabin door opened and Reuben stepped out, his wife behind him.

"Hannah?" The man's tone held a note of concern. He must have heard their raised voices.

Miss Grant spun toward Reuben. "All is well, I was simply explaining to Mr. Peak that it would be better for Itu to come with us so we can care for her."

Reuben's brow lowered, then he shifted his gaze to Nathaniel, his face a question.

Nathaniel eased out a pent-up breath. Looked like the man would hear both sides before answering. Surely that meant Reuben would see reason and convince Miss Grant of it.

He forced his voice to steady. "I think it's best she stay here. Her people will return for her, and I don't speak the language, so I won't be able to tell them where she is before they run a knife through me. Also, the doctor said she shouldn't be moved. I don't mind caring for her. She's my responsibility. She was found in my barn."

Reuben was silent for a long moment, his eyes never leaving Nathaniel's face. It was impossible to read his thoughts. At last, he glanced at his wife, a silent message passing between them. Then he turned to Miss Grant, and his voice gentled. "Hannah, I think she should stay here. All of Nathaniel's reasons are valid."

"But can he give her the care she needs?"

Nathaniel had never seen Miss Grant this worked up. Even when they were setting the girl's broken bone, she'd maintained a calm that he'd envied. Why did she care so much about this child? A stranger.

For that matter, why did *he*?

He didn't have time to stop and examine his reasons now. He just knew in his gut he needed to do everything he could for the girl. *He* needed to do it, not foist her off onto the neighbor women.

A slow awareness crept over him, realization that all three pairs of eyes were fastened on him. Had they asked him a question? He ran back through the last words in his mind. Miss Grant asked whether Nathaniel could give the girl the care she needed.

He nodded firmly. "I'll do everything I can for her. Including"—he cut his gaze to Miss Grant—"making sure she eats as much as she wants." This was all a little ridiculous. They had the same goal—for Itu to heal and be as comfortable as possible in the process.

He softened his tone and his posture, locking his gaze with Miss Grant's. "I truly want to help her, just like the rest of you do. I'll do my very best, and you're welcome to come visit whenever you want." He motioned toward the cabin. "Just come in and make yourself at home with her."

Something in her posture eased, maybe in the line of her jaw. "You don't mind if I come any time?" Her voice sounded resigned.

He offered a touch of a smile. "Night or day."

Her sigh spanned the distance between them as she turned to the Scotts. "The doctor said to tell you he's in the barn preparing his horse. I'm going to stay with her a while. I'll be along before dark."

Reuben glanced at his wife, his expression turning uneasy. "I'll stay too. You can ride back to our place with Bryan."

Well, it looked like he'd have company again. His little cabin probably hadn't seen this much activity since it was built.

If they stayed with the girl, maybe he could at least check his cows once before night fell. This was going to be tricky keeping up with all his responsibilities.

He could only hope he hadn't taken on more than he could handle.

Chapter Nine

The irony of our situation has never escaped me. Yet it doesn't stop my longing.

~ Hannah

*I*f Hannah didn't know better, she'd have thought her mother was intentionally keeping her from going to visit Itu. The next day, Mama brought out Cathleen's wash tub and they scrubbed clothing and linens all morning, then made fresh lye soap in the afternoon. She seemed on a mission to accomplish everything she could for Cathleen while they were there.

And how long would they be staying? Papa hadn't wanted to estimate before they arrived, as he had no idea whether Reuben would accept him. But now that her parents were enjoying this time to get to know their new son and daughter, what did that mean for their departure date?

She couldn't leave before she saw Itu back to health.

And how could she do that if she didn't go see the girl? How had the child fared this first day with only Mr. Peak? The possibilities churned in her mind, and by nightfall, a knot had developed in Hannah's midsection. Tomorrow, she would go see for herself.

And she'd take some food so the pair had more to eat than beans and cornbread. That couldn't be healthy as the child's only diet. Nor the man's.

At the table the next morning, conversation drifted from her father's desire to ride to Butte for supplies to Reuben's cattle and the progress he'd made cutting hay for the winter. Reuben talked about his land and how he rotated the animals among pastures, all topics she was accustomed to discussing over a meal, given their own ranch.

But she couldn't keep her mind from straying to the little Indian girl lying in a cabin an hour's ride away.

During a moment when the talking had faded and only the sounds of forks scraping plates and steady chewing were heard, she looked to her mother. "I plan to visit Itu today, this morning, if you don't need me for something."

All noise ceased as the others looked at her. Papa's gaze penetrated all the way through her. She hadn't meant to become a spectacle, only to confirm her agenda for the day.

"Do you think that's wise, dear?" Mama's tone was gentle, yet the concern was hard to miss.

"She surely needs a friend to cheer her up, and Mr. Peak will need help with her."

"What exactly do you know about this man?" Papa turned this question to Reuben.

Her new brother met his gaze. "I met him the same day you all came, and I think I've told you all I know. He was in the cavalry four years but said he left because he didn't like all he was asked to do with the Indians. Before that, I think he said he hailed from Virginia. He seems a decent fellow, but..."

She'd better speak up if she was to have any say-so in this decision. "I'm perfectly able to handle myself around him. And I suspect he'll be eager to leave me stay with the child while he takes care of his work away from the cabin. It can't be easy watching her and trying to get a ranch started."

"I'll go over with her." Reuben spoke almost before her last word faded. "I should offer to lend a hand to get him settled anyway."

Her father studied Reuben, worry lines still furrowing his brow. "Are you sure?"

The younger man nodded, then took another bite of ham as though the matter were decided.

She wasn't thrilled that her new brother felt the need to babysit her, but she'd be happy for this conversation to end. "I'll be ready to leave soon after breakfast."

He nodded. And even though she didn't look at either of her parents, she could feel the strength of their gazes on her. At least neither objected. She wasn't sure what she'd do if they refused her.

Their family had always worked together. They had to in order to make a life in the Canadian mountains. Going against a direct request didn't feel right.

And her father. He wasn't bound by blood to love her or even put up with her. He could just as easily turn his back, say she wasn't worth his trouble.

She was glad they hadn't forbidden her to go see Itu. Her spirit yearned to know how the child was faring. To care for her—not just her body but her mind and emotions, too.

A half hour later, she and Reuben were on the trail. One thing about this new brother, he didn't waste much—neither time nor words. He'd efficiently saddled the horses and loaded the food supplies while she'd helped clean up from the morning meal.

Silence settled over them as they rode through the woody mountain terrain. She was used to silence. Usually she preferred it. But this quiet felt stiff and clumsy, as if he wasn't sure what to say around her.

The other day when they'd ridden home together, she'd been so weary, the quiet ride hadn't bothered her so much. But his reserve grated on her today.

What could she say to start him talking? In truth, she knew so little about this brother, and hadn't yet found anything they shared in common except for the fact that he wasn't a great conversationalist. Neither was she.

Thankfully, he spoke first. "Did you like growing up in Canada?"

Was that a note of longing in his tone? Maybe it had only sounded in her imagination. "The country's beautiful. Somewhat like this, but the area we live in doesn't have near as many trees."

He nodded, then paused before speaking again. "You have...two brothers? I mean..." His shoulders rose as though he was inhaling a breath. "We have two brothers?"

She swallowed. This must be so hard for him. Coming to terms with an entire family he never knew about. "Yes. Robert is twenty-one and Will is thirteen. They stayed behind to keep the ranch running. My uncles will help, of course."

"Uncles. Are they...?" His words dropped off. Maybe he wasn't sure how to ask whether they were on Papa or Mama's side. In other words, were they a relation to him, too, or only to her?

The best way to answer was probably to talk through each one. "Let's see, Papa has a sister and two brothers who live near us. The house next to ours belongs to Aunt Noelle and Uncle Daniel. She's Papa's sister, and she's also a journalist. They have two children—Eli and Lena. Then there's Uncle Seth and Aunt Rachel. He's one of Papa's youngest brothers. They have Andy, Patrick, and Ruth. Next door to them is Seth's twin brother Samuel. He and his wife, Moriah, have Cherry and Nat."

He slid a sideways glance at her. Maybe at the unusual names?

"Aunt Moriah is half-Indian. The Piegan tribe. I think Nat is named after her grandfather—short for something I can't ever remember."

He tipped his head. "We have Piegan in the family?"

She nodded. "By marriage."

His brow wrinkled as silence settled over them again. Yet this time she could tell he was deep in thought.

Finally, he spoke again. "Robert and Will, do they look like...our father?" The word *our* still made him stumble. "I mean, my eyes are blue but they're the same shape. And our stature."

She couldn't help but smile. "Yes, you and Papa bear a striking resemblance. The boys, too, except they're not quite as broad as you. Maybe because they're still young. Their eyes are just like Papa's."

He glanced sideways at her, seemed to be studying her. "Your eyes aren't the same. Brown, but a different shape." His tone held only curiosity, not censure. He was simply struggling to understand his new family.

Yet the reminder pressed hard in her chest. If he was to truly know their family, it was only fair he know everything.

She took a fortifying breath. "You're right. My eyes don't look like his because he's not my father by birth." She didn't look at Reuben as she spoke, but caught the sudden stiffening of his posture out of the corner of her eye.

"What do you mean?"

Now that she'd begun, she'd have to tell the full story. Except maybe just the shortened version. "When they met, Mama's first husband had died, and she was expecting me. My Uncle Joseph was traveling with her up to Canada. They're twins, too." She slid a look at him, and the word caught his attention as she expected it would. "They needed someone to show them the way, so Papa agreed, and they journeyed the rest of the way together. All three of them.

"By the time they reached Mama's aunt and uncle in the valley where we live now, Papa and Mama had fallen in love. I was born, and Papa took me as his own. Gave me his name."

She wanted to look at Reuben again but couldn't quite bring herself to. Did he realize the deeper reality in what she'd just said? Papa had given up Reuben and his sister for other parents to raise, but he'd taken her—a girl not his own flesh and blood—and raised her as his own. The other truth it brought to light was that she and Reuben were not truly brother and sister by blood.

Yet he *was* her brother. In every way that counted.

She needed to say something about what a changed man Papa said he'd become by the time he and Mama married. How he'd been so bitter before. Mired in the loss of his wife and children.

Maybe it wasn't her story to tell, but she could at least plant the seed.

Turning her gaze to her brother, she spoke. "Reuben, you should ask our father to tell you about the years after he left you and Nora. I don't think it was a good time for him, but you should ask him."

Her brother looked at her, his gaze swimming with a world of emotions. Not a look she'd seen on him before. At last, he nodded.

For the rest of the ride, he said little, but she didn't mind now. The wall between them was broken like winter ice in a water trough.

Little by little, she'd come to know this new brother. And now, she was actually looking forward to the journey.

The fine hairs on the back of Nathaniel's neck rose as he hammered the log against the side of the cabin wall. He paused mid-blow and looked around.

Someone was out there. He'd seen the trampled leaves just inside the edge of the woods.

They were probably watching even now. Should he go investigate? Thus far, the person hadn't attempted to come closer. At least, not that he could tell.

Whoever it was must have returned for Itu. They'd probably looked in the barn and, not finding her, now watched until they knew for sure what he'd done with her.

Should he bring the child out? Or show the stranger he knew of their presence and invite them in?

In truth, he didn't want them to come in, not if it meant they'd try to take the girl away. She was too injured to be moved, the doctor said. Nathaniel had been giving her all the teas and herbs Grant left for her, and the willow tea seemed to be taking the edge off her pain and helping her rest.

If she left with the person watching from the woods, she'd lose all that. Her leg would grow worse, and the infection could even kill her if it spread through her body.

He couldn't let that happen.

After driving the last few blows against the log, he turned, picked up his rifle and tools, and headed back into the house. Part of him simply needed to know for sure she was still there. That she'd not been absconded with.

Itu opened her eyes as he stepped inside, and her face brightened a little—enough to send a warmth through his chest.

He couldn't help a smile of his own. "Hey, there."

She responded with sounds in her own language. She had a sweet, tiny voice. If only he could understand what she wanted to tell him.

He walked to her and eased his weary bones down to kneel beside her. When he brushed the dark locks from her forehead, her skin felt warmer than usual. Was it time for more tea?

He glanced toward the shelf over the hearth as if seeing the various herbs would help him know what time it was. One day he'd cut a window in this room. When he could obtain glass.

He was pretty sure it was too early for more medicine, but perhaps she was hungry. Scrunching his fingers together like he was raising food to his mouth, he asked, "Eat? Hungry?"

She bobbed her chin once. It seemed she was always hungry. If only he had more to offer her than meat, beans, and cornbread. Even the beans were disappearing quickly. He should probably try to simmer a meat stew for their evening meal, although he wasn't sure what making that involved. Did he just fill a pot with roasted meat and water? He had no raw meat unless he went hunting this afternoon.

Which he couldn't do. Itu couldn't be left for the stranger lurking in the woods to come steal her away.

Perhaps it was his imagination, but the sound of horses drifted from outside. He pushed to his feet, rifle in hand, and stepped to the door. He'd replaced the frame and built a new door but had intentionally notched a crack between two wooden slats so he could see who was outside.

Indeed, two horses stopped in front of the cabin, and the flash of blue skirt sent a jolt through his pulse.

He'd been hoping Miss Grant would come but hadn't let himself expect her. He sent a grin toward Itu, then opened the door and did his best not to let his pleasure show too strongly on his face.

Miss Grant approached the cabin with Reuben trailing her, both of them carrying saddle bags that looked loaded down.

"Welcome." He opened the door wider and stepped aside so they could enter.

She gave him a smile that was almost sheepish, yet it lit her pretty face and made his chest tighten. This woman possessed something special, in looks, abilities, and something else that was hard to lay a finger on.

He'd need to do a better job of protecting himself if he planned to stay immune to her charms.

"We came to visit"—she lifted the saddle bag she carried—"and brought some food supplies, too."

He motioned toward Itu. "Come in. I think she's glad to see you."

The girl's face had lit up like a gas light, and Miss Grant moved straight to her. She deposited her bundle on the floor, then sat beside the bed pallet and took Itu's hand. Her voice was too soft for him to catch the words as she stroked the girl's hair, but the child seemed to take in her presence like a starving person would food.

"Hope you don't mind the comp'ny." Reuben spoke beside him, and Nathaniel tore his focus away from the females to glance at the man.

"Glad for it." He couldn't help looking back at the females. "I think she's even happier than I am."

Reuben chuckled. "I figured you haven't been able to leave the cabin much, so you might like a hand cutting hay or whatever you need to work on."

Nathaniel turned back to him, brows raised. He'd come to work?

The man met his gaze. "Hannah won't need us around as long as she's with that little one."

True. And the thought of a full afternoon of work— work that truly needed doing—along with another man to help, was almost too good to be true.

Yet… "I'd appreciate that a lot, but I'm not sure it's safe to leave them here alone. This morning, I found a spot of ground trampled behind some trees just outside the edge of the clearing. I think they're still watching the cabin."

Reuben turned to scan the trees through the open door. "They likely are. If all three of us leave, they'd probably come and take her back to their lodges."

"I thought of that, but the doctor said the infection's pretty bad in her leg. He may have to amputate to keep it from spreading through her body. If she leaves this place where she's receiving proper care, I'm afraid she won't make it."

Reuben leaked out a long breath, his gaze still focused out the door. "All right then. You go do what you need to. I'll stay with Hannah."

That was an offer he couldn't refuse, not with his cattle neglected and weeks' worth of work waiting for him in his pastures.

Chapter Ten

These temptations strike at my weakest. Yet, I must be strong.

~ Nathaniel

"I can handle myself with an Indian as well as you, Reuben Scott. There's no need for you to sit and watch over me." Hannah forced herself to stay calm, but this overprotectiveness was getting out of hand. "I meet Indians all the time when I'm out with our herds. Did I mention our aunt is an Indian? I know exactly how to be friendly and not show fear. And I know well how to use my rifle should the need arise."

She reached for her gun and drew it nearer where she was sitting. From the day her parents had given it to her on her twelfth birthday, she'd not left their home site without it.

Her brother's face looked uncertain. She couldn't blame him completely, as he'd not known her long enough to understand how competent she was. But honestly.

She pointed toward the door. "Go help Mr. Peak like you planned. He needs you a lot more than I do." It wasn't that she didn't want her brother's company. It was just that she couldn't stand him watching over her like she was helpless.

His gaze slid from her to the girl, then over to the rifle. Finally, he focused on her face again. "You won't leave the cabin for any reason?"

She nodded. "Just let me make sure we have enough water and firewood first, then I won't even open the door." If that made him feel better, it was a small concession.

A long breath slid out of him. "All right. I'll get the water and wood."

It was all she could do not to roll her eyes as he stood and reached for a pot to fill. She was accustomed to being the eldest, the one who gave the orders and worried when concern was called for.

Having an older brother now would take some getting used to.

Nathaniel's muscles ached as they rode back from the hayfield, but it was the good kind of hurt, the kind brought on by hard work on his own ranch. With Reuben by his side, they'd managed almost as much as he'd have accomplished in two days on his own.

The only thing that kept peace from settling over him was his worry for Hannah—or rather, Miss Grant. Since he'd heard Reuben use her given name several times now, it was getting harder not to think of her that way too. He liked the name. It seemed to suit her quiet strength.

Had she seen any sign of the Indians while they were gone? *Lord, let her not have had trouble with them.* Reuben didn't seem concerned, so Nathaniel was trying not to be either.

As they rode into the quiet clearing, a steady stream of smoke rose from the cabin's chimney. That was a good sign.

They rode toward the barn, and after dismounting, Nathaniel reached for the other man's reins. "I'll tie your horse while I put mine up. You can go on in and check Miss Grant."

Reuben didn't object, and his mouth held a grim line as he nodded and handed over the reins, then strode toward the house.

Nathaniel made quick work of stripping the saddle from Raven and settling her in a stall. He'd tie her out to graze after his guests left. No sounds came from the cabin as he strode across the ground between the buildings. The quiet should've eased his worries.

But the knot in his gut seemed to ball tighter with every step.

When he reached the door, he held his rifle secure and listened for a second before reaching for the latchstring. He almost knocked, but if Indians held them captive, he certainly didn't need to alert them of his presence.

Instead, he pushed the door open. His gaze went first to the pallet where Itu lay. The child was there, her eyes closed and a peaceful expression on her face.

"Shh..." Miss Grant stepped in front of him, pulling his gaze to her pretty face. A very near face. She pressed a finger to her lips, drawing his attention to her beautifully-formed mouth.

He forced his focus up to her eyes.

She cut her gaze to the pallet. "She's sleeping." Miss Grant stepped back and waved him in. "I've made chicken and dumplings. Are you hungry?"

It was that moment that the fantastic smell hit his nose, taking him back to Mama's kitchen when he'd come in from a long day working horses. His belly gnawed loud enough Miss Grant could probably hear it.

She moved toward his table, and he stepped inside the room, his eyes tracking her to the steaming pot. He'd never seen a more beautiful sight than that woman scooping out the savory goodness she was piling on plates. *Glory be.*

Rueben straightened from a bucket of water he'd been washing in, shook his hands dry, and settled into a chair at the table. Clearly, those should be Nathaniel's next steps, too. He'd been eating by himself and with a camp full of men for so long, he'd almost forgotten how to be civilized.

When he and Reuben were seated, Miss Grant settled plates in front of them. He could do little more than soak in the steam and the intoxicating aroma.

"I hope it's as good as all that."

He jerked his eyes open to catch the smile tugging at her lips. He hadn't meant to be quite so enraptured, but he'd been eating beans and cornbread at every meal for far too long.

He offered a sheepish smile. "It just smells so good. I haven't been this spoiled in a while."

"Shall we say a blessing?" Reuben's voice rumbled beside him.

A pang hit his chest. This was something else he'd not done in years. The habit had died away a few weeks after he signed up with the cavalry.

He dipped his head while Reuben half-spoke, half-whispered a short prayer. Though not long, his words seemed earnest. Not a rote repeating of something he'd memorized, but a real conversation with a friend.

After the "Amen," Nathaniel picked up his fork and held it reverently over a dumpling. Then he dove in and raised the bite to his mouth. Amazing. The rich brown sauce was different than what his mama had made, but, oh, he'd never tasted anything that pleased his tasters so well.

He raised his head to tell Miss Grant exactly how good the meal was, but she'd moved across the room and knelt beside the fire, stirring something in his kettle. "Aren't you going to eat with us?" He spoke in a whisper that hopefully wouldn't wake the child.

Miss Grant turned to him with a half-smile and a shake of her head. That seemed to be the only answer she planned to give, maybe because she was trying to be quiet.

Still, he couldn't squelch the disappointment. Having her at the table would have been half his enjoyment in the meal, no matter how satisfying the food.

He could feel the weight of Reuben's regard on him, so he dipped his face back down to his dish and loaded another forkful. No sense in this man thinking Nathaniel had intentions toward Miss Grant.

He didn't. No matter how attracted he was to the woman, there was no room in his life for a time-consuming romance.

Having an injured child had already turned his plans upside down.

At last. Hannah guided her gelding over the path that was becoming a regular trail, as much as they'd traveled back and forth. And she was finally traveling it alone, a much needed respite from being constantly surrounded by people in the Scotts' cabin.

She loved her family, certainly. But she could only handle so much together time before her nerves worked themselves into knots.

This bit of peace with only her horse and the nature around her was exactly what she needed to regain her perspective.

A few minutes into the ride, Sterling's ears perked, and his muscles tightened under her saddle.

"What is it, boy?" She gripped her reins tighter but forced her legs to loosen so she didn't clamp the animal around the sides. She had her rifle in its scabbard, but she wouldn't reach for it unless whatever the horse saw proved a threat.

Through the trees ahead, a motion of brown shifted. Several bodies. A flash of white gave her an idea of what the animals probably were. She reached down to pat the gelding's shoulder. "It's all right, boy. Just deer."

This would be a prime opportunity to restock Reuben's meat supply if they needed it, but she was pretty sure his brother and sister-in-law had as much as they could eat.

What of Mr. Peak? He certainly needed more food, but his needs were along the lines of flour and milk and eggs. Which was why she'd brought the two latter ingredients from Cathleen's larder. He'd have to secure the rest of his needs from Butte.

The deer perked their heads as she and Sterling gave them a wide berth. A nice herd of seven or eight, with two fawns just losing their spots. Seeing God's creations in the wild like this always sent a thrill through her.

Sterling eased back into his normal stride as they continued on, and she let her mind wander to their destination. How was Itu faring today? Had Mr. Peak seen any more signs of the girl's family?

It seemed harsh to keep her away from them, but Hannah shared his concern that they would take the child away without the means to give her proper care. The thought that she might die of her injuries squeezed a hard knot into Hannah's throat, raising tears to sting her eyes.

Her gelding sprang to attention again, staring hard into the distance. Horses were as good as any guard dog, that was for certain.

She squinted to see what had raised Sterling's notice. Finally, a movement in the trees ahead snagged her gaze. Not an animal this time. At least, not only an animal.

The horse approaching in the distance carried a rider.

She kept Sterling moving toward the oncoming person but raised her rifle onto her lap so she'd have easy access. Not that she planned to use it, but she'd learned long ago that you never knew what kind of people you'd run into wandering in the mountain wilderness. Keeping a gun handy was simply a wise practice, especially for a woman.

As the stranger neared, she finally got a clear look at him. His buckskin clothing wasn't unusual, nor the fact that he rode a mule. Those sure-footed animals could be helpful on the rocky terrain. The bright red hair poking out from under his leather hat was a bit unusual, especially when matched with his boyish face.

They both reined to a stop when near enough to speak. He raised his hat just enough so she could see daylight over the top of his copper locks. "How-dy." His voice held a higher pitch than most men's, and rose even shriller on the last syllable. An odd way of speaking, but maybe he lived alone in the mountains without much chance to socialize.

She nodded a greeting. "Hello." There was no need for a long conversation, but he looked like he had more to say.

He propped a wrist on the front of his saddle. "I'm lookin' fer a town around here. You'uns know where it's at?"

"You mean Butte?" That was the only organized settlement she knew of, but she was hardly a local expert.

He tilted his head, and something about the look made her wonder if he was a few logs short of a wall. "Maybe. Jest lookin' fer folks."

Hmm... She turned back to the path she'd been riding. "If you follow this trail a half hour or so, it'll run into a wagon road. I think Butte is about five hours' ride if you stay on those tracks." Probably not the best directions, but he should see Reuben's cabin when he reached the wagon trace. He could ask for better details there.

Or maybe it was better he didn't. Pa and Reuben had gone to cut hay in a lower pasture, leaving Ma, Cathleen, and the elder Mrs. Scott at the cabin. She'd hate for this fellow to unnerve them.

Without another word, the man lifted his hat again—apparently in farewell—then shook the reins at his mule. "He-re we go." He spoke the words with that same high-pitched tone.

He seemed to be mumbling to himself as he passed but didn't spare her another glance.

She couldn't help watching him ride away. An interesting creature, to say the least.

The rest of the ride was blessedly uneventful, and as she rode into the clearing where Mr. Peak's forlorn cabin sat, she started up a whistle so he'd know she was there. At least the house didn't seem to lean anymore. And she'd noticed the new door and frame when she and Reuben were there the day before.

Now it just needed a good cleaning—and a wood floor.

She'd almost begun sweeping away the cobwebs and leaves littering the corners the day before but had contented herself with Itu and cooking the meal. Today, she may not exercise so much restraint. As tidy as Mr. Peak seemed to keep his person, she would have expected him to care a little more about his surroundings.

There were still so many things she didn't know about him.

As she scanned the yard, a head popped up from the barn roof. Even though she was trying to spot him, the sudden motion in the place she least expected made her heart surge. *Steady there, Grant.*

"Hello." He waved, then disappeared again. Must be repairing the roof up there. She'd noticed the barn leaked in several places that day they found Itu.

She rode toward the structure, and Mr. Peak strode out from behind it as she reined her gelding to a halt. When she slid to the ground, he reached for her reins.

"I didn't expect company again so soon." His face wore a smile, but his gaze seemed tired. Maybe it was simply that she was standing near enough to see the creases at the edges of his amber eyes. Even weary, those eyes had the power to hold her.

Chapter Eleven

So much to accomplish. My God-given nature won't allow me to ignore it.

~ Hannah

Hannah forced herself to turn away from Mr. Peak's gaze, not hand over her reins as he'd asked. Instead, she focused on untying her saddle bags. "I brought more food supplies and thought I could entertain Itu while you do your work."

"I'd appreciate that." His voice rumbled behind her. "She's been sleeping a lot today, but I think her pain's still pretty bad. She was crying in the night."

"Poor girl." She turned to see if she'd find more in his expression than his words gave away. Those were definitely dark shadows under his eyes. "Was she awake all night?"

He turned so she couldn't see his face well. "A lot of it. I'll settle your horse if you wanna go on in."

"I can do it. I didn't come to give you more work." She led Sterling into the open barn door, scanning the inside as her eyes grew accustomed to the dimness. "Getting the roof patched?"

He followed her inside. "I hope so. The roofs on both buildings need all new shakes, but I don't have time for that right now. Not until I get the hay cut and stored." He did sound tired. Weary.

"Do you plan to hire someone to help you through the summer?" She glanced back at him as she loosened the horse's girth.

He shrugged. "I don't know anyone who'd be willing to help. Honestly, I've only met Reuben and O'Hennessey, and both of them seem to have their hands full with their own ranches."

The thought entered her mind that her father was available, but he'd probably prefer to stay close to Reuben, helping where he could there. Of course, *she* wasn't nearly as occupied. She may not be as quick at felling trees as her brothers, but she could swing a scythe or a hammer as well as Robert or Will.

Of course, she and Mr. Peak couldn't *both* leave Itu all day. Aside from her awful injuries, the child couldn't be more than five or six.

Maybe, while he was out working with the stock and the hay, she could accomplish tasks around the house and barn. It wasn't too late to plant a garden either if she started right away. That would provide much-needed foodstuffs to last him through the winter.

But something kept her from opening her mouth. Probably the likelihood that he'd protest any offer she made. She'd just do the work and see if he noticed.

She held her tongue as she released Sterling into a stall, then walked beside Mr. Peak toward the house. He was taller than she remembered, and the strength of his presence beside her made her stomach flip.

What was she doing alone with this man? Maybe Mama had been right to wear such a concerned expression when she rode away that morning. But he'd shown himself to be honorable so far, and she fully expected him to ride out to work as soon as he saw her to the house.

Besides, she had her rifle, and knew well how to use it—as a gun or club or anything else required.

Yet his posture remained respectful as he allowed her to precede him into the house. And when she knelt by Itu's side, he remained a courteous distance away.

The girl's eyes fluttered open at Hannah's approach, although they seemed to hang heavy. Her mouth curved in a faint smile, but it appeared like the look could turn to tears at any moment.

"Oh, honey." She clasped one tiny hand and bent low to press a kiss to the child's temple as she brushed the hair away.

Hot. The fever was consuming her tiny body.

Hannah reached for the cup sitting beside the bed pallet and raised it to her nose to see if she could decipher the contents.

"That's willow tea. I've been giving it to her more often than the other herbs to help with her pain. I don't know if it's working or not." Mr. Peak had his hands clasped in front of him as though he was nervous—or worried.

119

The drink would help her, but tepid willow bark tea could unsettle the stomach. And the last thing Itu needed with all her other troubles was to cast up her accounts. Hannah shifted toward the hearth and opened the kettle to check its contents. "I'm going to pour it back in to re-heat. If taken cold, this tea can roil the stomach. Do you have any clean water for drinking?"

"In this pail." He stepped forward and lifted a bucket from beside the fire.

She scooped a cupful and returned to the girl's side. "Can you drink?" She kept her voice soft, but spoke clearly. She'd been teaching Itu a few words the day before, with *drink* being one of them.

The child lifted her head a tiny bit, and Hannah slipped a hand behind to help her. The girl only managed a couple of sips before she lay back, too weary to drink any more. She seemed to be getting worse, not better.

Hannah moved down to the broken leg. Doc Bryan had wrapped the splint all the way up to the knee, and she didn't expect to see anything unusual above that point. But she should check, just in case this new pain and exhaustion signaled the limb had worsened.

She peered under the bandage around the knee. The skin underneath had turned a bluish-red, and was still quite swollen. Was the bandage helping or hurting the leg? What little she could see looked horribly painful.

She scanned the rest of the bandage. If only she could see underneath. If only she knew what to do to fix the injuries. If only she could make this all better for the precious child.

Pulling the blanket back up, she wrapped Itu in a hug, careful not to hurt her tiny limbs. *Heal her, Lord. Touch her body and make her well.* Tears sprang to her eyes, unbidden and unwelcome.

"Is there anything I can do?" Mr. Peak's voice came to her in a low murmur, filled with enough concern that she knew he cared for the child too.

She sat up, sniffing back the moisture trying to slip through her defenses. "No. I'll stay with her today. You can do what you need to with your cattle and hay." She looked over at him, trying to summon an encouraging smile.

His earnest gaze nearly undid her. He sat on his haunches, his hands clasped in front of him, leaning forward as though he were ready to do whatever she asked. "Can I get you anything before I leave? More water? Do you want the fire hotter?"

She glanced toward the hearth. He already had a pile of wood in the corner, so she shook her head. The encouraging smile was a little easier to find this time. "Go do your work, Mr. Peak. We'll be fine."

"Call me, Nathaniel. Please." His face shifted into a grimace. "My last name reminds me too much of my days in the cavalry, and I'd just as soon forget that time."

What exactly did he mean by that? Had he done things he regretted? She studied his eyes, looking for some sign of his true feelings. All she could find was a well of earnestness that she could drown in if she let herself.

At last, she nodded. "All right. Call me Hannah. With only family around, I'm not used to being Miss Grant either."

His mouth teased in the hint of a smile, and he extended a hand. "Pleasure to meet you, Hannah."

He seemed to realize immediately what he'd done, and red crept into his face. He pulled his hand back, rubbing it across his belly. "I guess ladies don't shake, do they? I've been out of the general population too long."

His boyish embarrassment almost pulled a grin from her. She extended her own hand. "I'm pleased to meet you, Nathaniel."

When he closed his hand around hers and gave a single shake, his grip was solid, yet not too tight. Warm, and the touch of his skin against hers sent a tingle up the length of her arm.

Not a sensation she'd meant to feel.

She pulled back and turned away as soon as she could do so without being rude. She needed to do a better job of keeping her distance from this man.

Hannah rose from her chair at the dinner table that night to retrieve the apple pie her mother had baked. Hannah was usually the one who did the baking in the family, but since she'd been with Itu all day, Mama had accomplished the task.

"I've been thinking it's time we ride down to Butte for supplies." Her father's voice filled the table as she cut slices of the dessert. "Hannah's eager to see the sights, too."

Her chest tightened. She *had* been eager. Still wanted to. But now was hardly the time to leave Itu and Nathaniel alone. The girl had been in so much pain that day. Several times when Hannah thought she was sleeping, she'd heard tiny sobs drifting from the blankets. The sounds were enough to break her heart.

Maybe if they went to Butte soon, she could ask the doctor to come back early. It was still four days before the end of the week when he'd promised to check on Itu, but she wasn't sure the girl could wait that long. She'd definitely taken a turn for the worse.

"When are you planning to go?" She tried to keep her tone nonchalant.

"Do you have any work for me these next few days?" Her father looked over at Reuben.

The man shook his head. "You've outworked me already. I'm sure Cathleen'll have a few things she needs from the mercantile if you don't mind picking them up."

Papa nodded. "Of course." Then his gaze went to her mother, and a silent conversation passed between them. A moment later, he looked to Hannah. "How about we leave in the morning?"

She eased out a breath. The sooner, the better for little Itu. She wouldn't have time to tell Nathaniel where she'd gone, but surely they'd only be in town a night or two at the most.

And if Itu didn't get help soon, she might lose that leg. Or maybe her life.

Chapter Twelve

It's funny the things God uses to guide us.

~ Hannah

Butte was nothing like what Hannah expected.

As they rode through what must have been the main street, she could only stare at the long rows of buildings. Not made of rough logs like the structures in Fort Hamilton, these were mostly built of milled wood with some covered in whitewash. Faded whitewash, with thick coats of dust and mud that made the paint look like more of a dirt-wash.

Her father drove the wagon—Reuben's rig that he insisted they bring to make hauling supplies easier—down the building-lined road, slowing for a woman and two children who were crossing just ahead.

A long white building on the left caught her focus. Or rather the sign above the door that read *Doctor's Clinic*. This must be where Doc Bryan and Cathleen's other brother worked.

She pointed to the structure. "Can we stop there so I can ask them to go up and check Itu?" She'd already filled her parents in on the girl's worsening condition.

Papa didn't show any sign of slowing the rig. "Let's find the hotel first and get the animals settled. Then we can go visiting."

Her body itched to jump down and stride toward the building, but she clutched the wood bench to keep herself in place. Surely it would only take a half hour or so to accomplish those tasks. Cathleen had sent a bundle of things for her sisters-in-law and niece and nephew, so Mama would surely want to come along to the clinic.

The hotel where they took rooms was grander than she'd expected. In fact, she'd never been inside a building that contained a second floor like this one. The staircase railing had a beautiful carving that would have done well with a coat of polish. Their own little cabin in the mountains might be rustic compared to this, but she and her mother kept it neat and as clean as possible, a habit the proprietors of this establishment would do well to adopt.

Not that the place was overly dirty. Especially not compared to the way Nathaniel's cabin had been before she set to work on it the day before. But it was hard not to judge the character of the owners by the dirt in the corners and dust covering the furniture.

Of course, she could handle a little dirt given the fact she had her very own room again. She'd missed this luxury since they'd come to Reuben and Cathleen's.

126

A soft knock sounded on her door, and she pulled it open to find both her parents standing in the hall. Mama looked refreshed with her hair re-coifed and a gentle smile on her face. Papa just looked like Papa—the same no matter what time of day or season of the year.

"Shall we go eat before we visit Cathleen's family?" Her mother's smile turned hopeful. "We saw a little café on the way to the clinic."

Another delay? Maybe she should walk to Doc Bryan's place while her parents ate. But the thought of dining in a real café was sorely tempting. Especially when they reached the building and the tantalizing aroma of stewed beef and something sweet drifted through the doorway.

Two men were exiting the place, one who appeared to be near her father's age, and one who might have been young, although his scruffy beard and worn flannel shirt made him look almost as old as the other. She hadn't seen many people since they entered the town, probably because it was still mid-afternoon and most men would be working. But she'd not been very impressed with those she had seen.

Still, she offered these men a smile as they nodded a greeting in passing.

Inside the café, the savory aroma grew stronger. The place appeared neat and cheery, with long tables lined on either side of a center aisle. A few men sat around the room, either leaning over plates or lounging in conversation with each other.

127

An apron-clad woman strode from one table to another, refilling cups with the pitcher she carried. When she turned to send them a welcoming smile, her beauty nearly caught Hannah's breath. Those dark eyes were captivating, along with the soot-black hair and elegant features. She didn't look like she belonged in this town of less-than-promising men.

"Hello. Take a seat anywhere you like." She motioned toward a couple of empty tables. "We're serving stewed beef and potatoes this evening. Can I get you plates?"

"Yes, please." Mama's voice held all her normal grace.

Papa motioned toward an empty table, and they sat on the bench seats lining either side.

There was only one person nearby, and he turned as they settled themselves. "I haven't seen you folks in Aunt Pearl's before." He extended a hand.

Papa took the offering. "Just arrived in town today."

A flash of pleasure lit the man's blue eyes, and his gaze slid to Hannah before jerking back to her father. "Newcomers. Good to meet you. I'm Harvest Jenkins."

Papa nodded. "A pleasure. I'm Simeon Grant, and these are my wife and daughter."

The man's gaze wandered back to Hannah, and she met it head-on. He looked to be only a few years older than she was, maybe thirty-five at the most. Clean-cut, and handsome in a smooth, tailored way. Except for that mustache, which cluttered up his face. In truth, she'd rarely seen men who dressed like him, with a cutaway coat and necktie. Was he a businessman in town?

"Here you are."

The arrival of the dark-haired woman with their food shifted Hannah's attention back to her table. As her parents conversed with the woman, then continued their casual discussion through the meal, she couldn't help stealing a few more glances at Mr. Jenkins.

He was handsome like Nathaniel, but in a different way. This man seemed so…smooth. Like he knew well who he was and what he wanted. Nathaniel also had a confidence about him, but it came through in the earnest expression of his eyes, the way he truly listened to a person, the way he put his all into everything he did. He wasn't afraid to show his passion, but he also knew when to hold his tongue.

When she'd first met Mr. Nathaniel Peak, she'd been waiting to see his true colors. She was finally coming to realize that he didn't hide himself behind a façade. He truly was a hardworking man who cared about others and wasn't afraid to put himself fully into whatever he set his mind to.

The kind of man who'd take in an injured Indian child and exhaust himself to care for her, setting aside his own needs to ease her pain as well as he could.

A longing swelled inside her to be with them, to talk with Nathaniel while she cradled Itu in her arms. The ache of her need swelled inside her chest so strong it brought tears to her eyes. She dropped her gaze to the plate, forking another bite of potato to distract herself.

Tomorrow. Her father had promised they would return to Reuben's tomorrow if they could get all the supplies they needed in the morning.

Lord willing, she'd see Nathaniel and Itu the next day. *Help them, Lord. Be with them even when I can't.*

Tomorrow couldn't come soon enough.

Nathaniel knelt beside Itu's bed pallet, brushing the backs of his fingers across her forehead. She was so hot and had slept much of the day. He'd thought that last part would help her, especially since she couldn't seem to rest much at night. But her fever seemed to be rising.

"Can you drink a little more of this?" He slipped his hand behind her head to raise it.

Her eyes barely squinted open, but at least she was awake and able to sip a little. He'd reheated the willow tea like Hannah said to do and given the girl everything else exactly as often as Simeon Grant had instructed.

Yet nothing seemed to be helping. He'd prayed Hannah would come again today—actually bowed his head and petitioned the Almighty. Her presence seemed to give Itu strength. It certainly brought them both comfort. She didn't even have to clean or cook like she had the day before, although stepping into that clean cabin after she'd left had stirred his soul in a way he could still feel.

But truly, all she had to bring was herself and that beautiful spirit that lit a room when she stepped into it.

Yet she hadn't come. Maybe tomorrow. *Lord, let her come tomorrow. We need help.*

Hannah breathed in the cool mountain air as she stepped outside later that evening. With her mind churning so much, she needed a walk. Maybe her angst was leftover emotion from talking to Doc Bryan, or urgency to get back up the mountain now that he would accompany them to Reuben and Cathleen's tomorrow, then on to see Itu. Maybe this turmoil was her worry for the girl.

Or maybe this unrest was simply exhaustion from meeting so many new people. Bryan had introduced her to his wife and daughter, then his brother, Alex, and his wife and son. She already loved them all—Cathleen's family, which became their own by extension. Yet being around so many new faces had taken the rest of her energy.

A few moments to herself was what she needed, outside where she could see the mountains rising up in the distance around the town.

She turned opposite the direction they'd walked earlier that day. She wasn't sure exactly what lay this way, but she could see a few lights in the buildings as evening began to settle over the place. It seemed like many storekeepers lived in the back part of their shops, which made sense.

Every so often, she passed a person walking along the boardwalk. Several looked like weary miners returning home or maybe doing business after their work ended. Doc Bryan and his brother had told them a little about the mines around town and how the working conditions were especially hard. A look at the soot-covered men she passed made her heart squeeze. Surely there was something to be done that would make their work easier.

"Miss Grant?"

She spun to face the voice. Who would know her name here? A man stepped into the light from a nearby window, and she caught the glimmer of buttons on his coat, as well as the dark contrast of his mustache against his lighter skin.

"Mr. Jenkins." Her heart thudded in her chest, and she inhaled a deep breath to slow her pulse. It was only the friendly man from the café.

He stepped up beside her with a slight bow. "'S a pleasure to see you again." His words didn't hold the same crispness as they had earlier but seemed to slur a bit.

She tipped her head to look at him from the corner of her eye. He was smiling at her, but the look was off-kilter, one side of his mouth rising more than the other.

And his breath. She knew that noxious odor the moment it brushed her nose. One couldn't enter Fort Hamilton without detecting the strong odor of whiskey.

She stepped back. "Good to see you again, sir. I was just going back to our hotel." More than one encounter with a drunken trapper had taught her to leave them be. Men who touched the stuff were unreliable at best and often downright dangerous.

"With me a while." He grabbed her arm, his speech even more slurred than before. "I don't usually have a pretty lady to pass the lonely, lonely..." He paused, apparently struggling to find the right words. Or maybe he'd lost his line of thought altogether.

She pulled back, twisting her arm to try to remove it from his grasp. As drunk as he was, his grip was firm. "Thank you, but *no*." She barked the last word, just in case he was having trouble hearing in his inebriated state. "Release me, please." She'd ask nicely first, then get as forceful as she had to.

He tugged her forward. "Come on, Miss Grant. Tell me about yourself. Such a pretty"—he hiccupped—"thing."

She walked beside him, more to keep her balance than anything as she bent down and reached under her skirt, extracting the hunting knife from its sheath in her boot. With a flick of her wrist, she gripped the handle and pressed the blade against the man's neck. "I said, *release me*. Now."

He took twice as long to react as any sober man would, but he finally stopped, his eyes spreading wide as he leaned his head back. She kept the blade pressed against him with her free hand and tugged her arm where he held her.

His hand dropped away, both arms dangling by his sides.

"Good night, Mr. Jenkins." She backed away, making sure she was several paces away before she turned and took long strides toward the hotel.

From the corner of her eye, she watched for movement on the boardwalk that signaled he was following her. He probably hadn't premeditated his attack, but foul drink was poison to a man's character.

Finally, the hotel came in sight. As she slipped through its door into safety, she breathed a thankful prayer heavenward. Once again, God had proved His faithfulness to her.

Lord, protect Itu the same way. She needs it even more than I do.

Chapter Thirteen

How can this be right when everything about it feels wrong?

~ Nathaniel

Two days now.

Hannah hadn't come for two days, and Nathaniel's nerves were strung tight enough to ignite gunpowder. Itu's fever was burning ferociously. She was almost incoherent most of the time. He was afraid to leave her side except for quick trips to tend Raven or retrieve fresh water.

They needed help.

If Hannah wouldn't come to them, he'd have to go get her. And maybe he needed more than just her. In truth, they needed the doctor. His gut said the doctor would have to follow through on that awful possibility he'd mentioned the first time he came.

"Oh, Itu." The words slipped out as he stroked her sweat-dampened hair. "I'm going to have to leave you for a little while to get help. But I'll be back. Wait for me. I'll be back soon."

The girl didn't stir, just breathed in another raspy breath through her chapped lips. Should he take her with him? She'd get help quicker, but her body seemed so frail, he wasn't sure she could survive the trip. Especially not on horseback.

He leaned down and pressed a kiss to her forehead. "Hold on until I return."

Without taking the time to saddle Raven, he slipped on a bridle and pulled himself up bareback.

They covered the distance as quickly as the winding trail through the woods allowed. One day he'd cut a road through here so they could travel with a team and wagon. Of course, that would only be helpful when he actually had a wagon.

So much held a higher priority than buying a rig though. And the most important of all—Itu's life.

Urgency swept through him as he cantered into Reuben's yard. A wagon and team sat beside the house, and another horse had been tied to the hitching rail. Did the man have more company? It didn't seem many more people could fit inside that little cabin.

But the horses hitched looked familiar, like the ones he'd seen in Reuben's corral. Maybe they'd been to town.

Two figures were working around the wagon, and it wasn't hard to make out the tall form of Simeon Grant. But then the second man came into better view, and Nathaniel had to blink to figure out what he was seeing. They couldn't both be Simeon.

No, the second man was Reuben. Yet their outlines were so similar, they could easily be father and son.

Hadn't they been strangers that day he'd first come to meet his new neighbors? He'd sure thought so, but maybe he'd been mistaken. That would account for why the Grant family had stayed here so long.

Not that he was complaining. Their presence sent a flood of relief through him.

He reined in near the wagon, and both men came to him with worry clouding their features.

"The girl is much worse. Any chance you can come? I've done everything I know to do, but she's burning with fever and not very alert." He directed his comments to Simeon, but he was really talking to anyone who would listen. They needed help.

Reuben moved toward the house. "Bryan just got here. We'll come now."

Bryan...the doctor? His relief nearly swept the strength from his muscles. His gaze moved back to Simeon, who was watching him.

"We just returned from Butte. Hannah told Bryan how the child was worsening, so he agreed to ride back with us."

Hannah had done this. The urge slipped through him to take her in his arms and swing her around in a tight hug. That would be unacceptable, especially with her father standing here, eyeing him. But he'd sure say thank-you.

Simeon turned toward the house. "I'll see if he needs me to bring anything, then we'll saddle the horses."

137

Nathaniel helped with what he could, but there seemed precious little he could do to speed the process of getting everyone ready to head back to his place. In the end, Doc Bryan, Simeon, and Hannah saddled their horses to ride back with him.

Hannah's face was a mask of worry as she exited the barn with her gelding and saw him standing with his horse. "How is she?"

He swallowed down the lump that tried to clog his throat. "Not good." He relayed the same details he'd told her father, plus the things he'd been doing to help.

She mounted and moved closer to him. "I'm so sorry I haven't been there to help. My parents wanted to go to Butte for supplies, and I thought it might be good for me to go along and see if the doctor would come back with us." Her jaw set firmly as her gaze lifted toward the trail to his cabin. "I should have been with Itu, though."

Oh, how he wished she'd been here. But really, her decision had been the right one. "Thank you for bringing the doctor."

The barn door opened again, and Simeon stepped out with his paint mare, followed by Doc Bryan.

Nathaniel mounted Raven and turned the mare homeward. "Let's go."

Lord, don't let us be too late.

Hannah's heart felt like it might be breaking as she wrapped her arms around Itu's tiny body. The child was as hot as a warming stone just pulled from the fire. At least she seemed to be aware that Hannah was there, although she'd only slitted her eyes once in response to the kiss Hannah pressed to her forehead.

Doc Bryan had removed the splint and was now unwrapping the bandage that covered the girl's leg below the knee. Hannah forced her body to remain still, not to react to what would surely be an awful sight.

Nathaniel knelt on the side opposite the doctor, and her father was positioned by the girl's feet, both men ready to assist should Bryan need anything. But what could they do now? The real work would come if Itu's leg had to be removed.

God, no. Save this child from that torment. She wasn't even sure how it would be done, but the process could be nothing less than excruciating.

As Bryan peeled away the soiled bandage, Itu's swollen and bruised leg came into full view. Hannah had to press her lips shut to keep from casting up her accounts at the hideous assortment of reds, blues, yellows, and greens. But it was the gash above the ankle that tightened her stomach into a sick knot. Could there be a more grotesque wound? No wonder a fever raged inside the poor child's body.

She ducked low over Itu's face, stroking her hair and cheek. She wanted to hum to the girl to soothe her, but she didn't want to distract Doc Bryan's focus. A glance at him showed his attention honed on the wound. When he touched the swollen edge of the gash, Itu jerked and clawed for his arm.

Nathaniel caught her hand before she could grab the doctor, then he took both of her little hands in his big, workworn palms, stroking his thumb across them.

Doc Bryan looked up at them, his gaze shifting from one adult to the next. "The only thing we can do is take it off."

A sob caught in Hannah's throat, slipping out against her will. Not this sweet child. How much horror could her tiny body withstand?

A hand settled on her shoulder, stroking. Nathaniel's hand. She turned to meet his eyes and saw a match to her turmoil there.

"If we take the leg off now, I think we can save her life." The doctor's words broke through her pain.

They both turned to face him, but thankfully, Nathaniel didn't pull his hand from her shoulder. She needed the strength of his touch.

"If we don't get rid of this infection, she'll probably only live another few days. At the most."

Hannah clamped her jaw against another sob, putting her focus into stroking Itu's hair with as gentle a touch as she could maintain. She wanted to scream. To cry. To scoop up the girl and take her away from this misery.

But she could do none of it.

Her gaze lifted to Nathaniel again. They had no choice. Did they?

His thumb stroked the ridge of her shoulder. "If it will save her, we have to." His eyes were rimmed in red, but in their depths, she saw his determination. His will to see Itu through this no matter what it cost him.

She would do the same. No matter what it cost.

The doctor took a couple minutes to ready his tools, and she had to look away when he pulled a hideous-looking saw from his bag. Finally, he turned back to them. "I'll let her smell the chloroform, and she'll fall asleep while I remove the leg. I'll need everyone out at that point except Mr. Grant." He looked to Papa.

Part of her wanted to object. She should be here for Itu. What if the girl woke partway through the surgery? What if something happened and the doctor needed an extra hand?

But in truth, she wasn't sure she could stomach watching what was about to happen. Not to sweet Itu.

She'd developed the ability to separate herself from an animal when hunting so she could remove the organs to get at the meat and cut off the hide to provide blankets for their family. But those were animals, not a child she'd loved and cared for. A girl who'd become part of her heart.

Yes, it was best she leave the cabin while the worst of the surgery took place.

After Bryan held a cloth near her face, Itu's breathing slipped into an even in-and-out. The doctor nodded at them, and Nathaniel rose. He moved to Hannah's side and took her arm to help her up.

She let him. Assistance she wouldn't normally need, but her legs felt like they might give way at any moment.

He touched the small of her back, guiding her toward the door, then shifted his hand to her elbow to help her up on the stoop, then down the other side. His nearness was a comfort she couldn't bring herself to push away.

Even if she should.

But she wasn't so sure about that now. The more she'd come to know Nathaniel, the more she appreciated his character. And what little she'd seen of the men in Butte had only reinforced those feelings.

Yet now was hardly the time to think on them. Not with what was happening just on the other side of the cabin door.

She blew out a long breath, trying to force out the tension locked in her chest. Nathaniel rubbed circles in her mid-back, and she leaned into him. Maybe she should say something, but what words would help? They could only wait.

By the time the cabin door opened, she was leaning against Nathaniel, and he'd wrapped a hand around her waist. Supporting her.

She straightened and turned toward the door. Papa stuck his head out, his face grim and maybe a little pale. "You can come back in. She hasn't woken yet."

When she stepped into the cabin, Hannah's gaze flew to the little form on the pallet of blankets, but it took a moment for her eyes to adjust to the dimness of the room.

A blanket had been pulled over the girl's body, and for a horrible second, Hannah's mind told her the worst had happened. But then she saw the tiny round face at the end of the covers. That face still held color.

Her feet moved forward before she could tell them to. But as she began to kneel beside the girl, Hannah's gaze slid down to her injured leg. The blanket lay limp from the knee down where the bulky splint had been just an hour before.

Bile rose in her throat, but she forced it down. Forced her focus back to the girl's sweet face. She stroked a soft cheek.

"When will she wake up?" Nathaniel's voice rumbled just behind her.

Hannah held her breath for the answer but didn't shift her focus from the child.

"Should be within the quarter hour. She'll be groggy for a while. And thirsty, but she should only have little sips of water at first so it doesn't come back up."

Hannah swallowed. "Will she be in a lot of pain?" How could she not be?

"Not much while the chloroform is still in her system. Her body will still be recovering from the infection, so we'll be working to bring the fever down. The leg will hurt at times, as though the injured part is still there. It won't be easy on her."

Hannah looked up at the doctor's face, trying to take in the full meaning of his words. "But she'll live?" She had to hear the verdict directly from him.

His eyes took on a gentleness she wanted to cling to. "She has a better chance now. But we'll have to see how she does over the next day or two."

A whimper brought Hannah's gaze down to the girl. Itu shifted her head. Hannah stroked the hair away from her face. "Are you ready to wake up, sweet one?"

Someone moved behind her, and a cup of water appeared by Hannah's side. It was another minute or two before the girl's eyes opened and her vision seemed to focus. She locked her gaze on Hannah, and Hannah didn't move away from her. Just stayed, holding her hand, stroking her arm or face or hair.

After a few more minutes, she was able to help Itu drink some water. The effort seemed to exhaust the girl, proving once more how little strength her body had left.

They would work on that, though. Everything that could be done to help this sweet child, she would do.

But God would have to handle the real work. *Lord, save her. Please. You have to.* Surely the loving God she served wouldn't take this innocent child so soon.

Chapter Fourteen

'Tis like finding my way in the dark.

~ Hannah

Nathaniel hesitated at the cabin door the next morning. Should he knock first?

Hannah and her father had volunteered to stay the night with Itu. And the doctor had offered as well. For propriety's sake, Nathaniel slept in the barn, but so many times he'd almost crept to the house to check on the girl.

Had she slept any better than the past few nights? Her fever had still raged through the evening, and he wasn't sure how much more her little body could take.

Help her, God. Please. Did the Almighty even hear these prayers he'd been sending up? He'd gone to church with his ma and grandma most of his life, but during his cavalry days, they weren't often settled in one place on Sundays for a chapel service. And even then, he'd not been very diligent to attend.

If he could go back and change that, he would. Anything to help God listen to him now.

Not for me, Lord. For that little girl.

He tugged on the latch string and eased the door open a crack, then paused to take in the scene as the sounds of light snoring drifted to him.

Itu lay on her bed pallet just as she had for days now. Her face had softened in sleep, a good sign. Maybe they'd fared better this past night than he had the nights before.

His gaze raised to the woman kneeling in front of the hearth, working over the pot. Her position outlined her slender form, the soft curves he could still remember holding yesterday as they'd waited for the surgery to finish.

He was coming to care for her more than he'd ever intended. But how could he not? She was strong and kind and beautiful, and the way she loved and tended this injured Indian girl had stolen his heart.

As though she could hear his thoughts, she turned to look at him.

He pushed the door wider, glancing at the sleeping doctor laid out along one wall. He'd probably learned to take what snatches of sleep he could get any time he could find them. Hannah's father must have already left the cabin.

Keeping his steps quiet, Nathaniel eased inside and pressed the door shut. Hannah watched him approach, and he studied her face for signs of how the night had gone. Dark shadows haunted her eyes, but her mouth curved a little.

He dropped to his haunches beside her, positioned so he could see both the fire and the sleeping girl. "How are you?" He kept his voice low and searched Hannah's gaze, those pretty brown eyes that showed him all the way to her soul.

She lowered her gaze, turning back to the pot she'd been working with. "I'm well. Are you ready for coffee?"

The way she wouldn't look at him when she answered told him a great deal. She was worried about the girl, and the thought made him wish he could take her in his arms. Pull the heavy weight of anxiety from her.

If only he were capable.

Instead, he turned to look at Itu again. "How is she?"

Hannah followed his focus. "She slept fitfully, but I think her fever may be lower this morning." She glanced at the doctor. "Maybe. We'll see what Doc Bryan says."

He reached forward and brushed the girl's forehead with the backs of his fingers. Maybe it wasn't as hot. He wasn't very good at assessing these things.

Turning back to the hearth, he peered inside the pot. "What can I do to help?"

"I'm only making a simple corn mush, but it's almost ready." She reached for the coffee pitcher and a cup, and poured a full helping of the dark, steamy brew.

He took the tin when she offered it, then cradled it between both his hands, savoring both the warmth and the aroma. "What's the plan for today?" A taste of the brew proved it was just as good as he'd suspected.

She reached for a bowl and scooped a spoonful of the creamy porridge. "If she doesn't take a turn for the worse, the doctor plans to leave this morning." She kept her voice barely louder than a whisper. "I'll stay with Itu today, and

147

Papa said he'd be glad to help you in the fields or with whatever you need doing." She handed him the bowl.

He lowered the half-empty coffee cup to the floor and took the warm gruel, raising it to inhale a good whiff. "All this good food alone might pull her through the infection."

Hannah raised her brows. "It's only corn gruel. I wish I had eggs and milk to make a real meal."

A bit of warmth touched his ears. But then, she'd seen his feeble supplies. He raised a bite of the porridge to his mouth to test its warmth. "I need to get a milk cow and chickens. I plan to, there's just so much still to do."

She watched him. "Are you looking for more stock cattle first?"

He swallowed down a hearty bite. "I have to get the hay cut first, or I won't have enough to feed the animals I have through the winter. I wanted to get started on my horse herd, but I think I may've been getting ahead of myself."

She tipped her head. "So hay first, then horses. You've fixed the barn roof and replaced the cabin door. What else is on your list?"

"A corral by the barn for the riding horses. A coop for chickens. I need to fell enough trees so I can cut them into slabs through the winter for a cabin floor. And furniture. But before that, I need to replace the chinking between the logs. A few more rains and I think half of it will wash away." He stared at the daylight filtering through a bare spot directly across from him.

Then he realized all he'd said aloud. "You didn't want to hear all that though." He took another bite to silence himself.

"I did actually." Her voice was still quiet but held a thoughtfulness that made him turn back to look at her.

Her gaze was intense. "I'd like to help."

He swallowed, wanting to look away. Wanting to deny his need. Yet, another part of him craved to pull her close. To kiss those lips that called to him. To tell her how much he truly needed her.

Instead, he said nothing. Just let her nearness, those beautiful eyes, speak to him.

The cabin door opened, breaking through his focus. He turned to see Simeon entering, the sound of his tread on the stoop stilling the snores coming from the doctor. It appeared his few quiet moments with Hannah were at an end.

Maybe that was for the best, but he couldn't help the frustration that slipped through him.

Hannah may not be a swift hand at cutting slabs of wood for corral fencing or floors, but she could chink cabin walls with the best of them. She'd certainly helped with her fair share of re-chinking projects at their cabin or one of their family members'.

The men had all gone their separate ways—the doctor to stop by Reuben's house before returning to town and Nathaniel and her father out to check the cattle, then work in the hay field. She'd cleaned up from the morning and swept out the cabin again, stopping to visit with Itu every time the girl was awake. She was able to get the child to drink some willow tea, but Itu shook her head every time Hannah tried to spoon corn gruel into her mouth.

Her body needed sustenance, but she surely felt too miserable to eat. Hannah would have to keep trying.

For now, though, it was time to mix some chinking mud and set to work. She'd packed lunches for her father and Nathaniel, so there was a chance she could get two or three walls patched before she had to stop to prepare the evening meal. Of course, that depended on how hard the old mud was to scrape out.

A few hours into the project, she stood in the warm summer sun sweating and covered in chinking material. Itu had slept with only one interruption, which was surely good for her. Mama always said sleep contained healing powers.

The old chinking mud between the logs fell out easily, but she'd forgotten exactly how long it took to do a thorough job.

And how much mud the task required. At this rate, she'd only get one long wall finished today.

But that was one wall Nathaniel wouldn't have to worry over. She scooped up another handful of the mud and grass mixture and pressed it into the crevice between two logs.

A sound from behind made her pause. It was only the snapping of a twig, but something about the noise made the fine hairs on the back of her neck stand on end. She eased around to study the trees around the clearing.

Nathaniel had said he'd seen evidence of someone watching from the woods, but that had been several days ago. With all the anxiety of yesterday, she'd forgotten to be on her guard.

Was someone standing out there now? Watching her?

She hadn't brought her rifle outside with her. *Foolish.* Were the Indians here friendly like the Piegan back home? Reuben had said he thought Itu was from the Hidatsa tribe, but she knew nothing about them.

Perhaps if she greeted the stranger in the woods, they could convince the person that Itu needed to stay here where she could be cared for adequately. Together, they could all help the child heal. Surely Itu would be overjoyed to see her family again.

Rubbing the mud from her hands, she stepped toward the trees, into the open land between the cabin and the woods. "Hello?" Maybe the stranger knew English, but maybe not. The only other greeting she knew was the Piegan welcome her aunt Moriah had taught her, so she spoke that.

Silence was her only answer. Long, uninterrupted quiet. No birds twittered. No chipmunks chattered. Someone was out there.

"If you'd like to come see Itu, I can take you to her." *Lord, don't let this be a mistake.*

She stood quietly. Waiting.

151

No shadows stepped from the trees. No movement at all that she could see. Maybe it would take some time for them to come to trust her.

With one final scan of the woods, she turned and strode back to the cabin, heading around to the front.

She'd feel better if she were there with Itu. And she could still work by trimming the chinking from inside.

Having Itu's family there would surely help the child, but no matter what, Hannah couldn't let her be taken. As weak as her body was, a journey would be the end of her.

And what would her people say when they saw her amputated leg? *God, help us.*

Even as she sent up the prayer, a knot balled tight in the pit of her stomach.

As Nathaniel lay on his sleeping pallet that night, his eyes traced the fresh chinking along the wall beside him. He still couldn't believe how much Hannah had accomplished. Couldn't quite fathom that she'd done it all.

Hannah Grant was one special lady, doing more in one day than he could manage in two or three.

Itu's thick breathing filled the quiet cabin. The girl's fever still burned, but she didn't seem quite as miserable as before her leg was removed. If they could get a decent night's sleep tonight—both of them—maybe he could manage to care for her the way she needed tomorrow.

Hannah hadn't said when she'd return, and he had to be able to manage without her.

He probably wouldn't accomplish much more than caring for the girl, what with the herbs and bandage changes she'd need, not to mention the food and lots of water the doctor had prescribed.

That wasn't half of what Hannah could manage, but he couldn't rely on her. As much as he was beginning to wish it, Hannah Grant wouldn't be in his life forever. He had to manage on his own two feet.

"You think she's getting better?" Hannah knelt beside her mother the next afternoon. Mama had been feeding warm chicken broth to Itu while Hannah put together the last of the evening meal.

"I think so." Mama's voice rang in a sing-song tone, probably for the girl's benefit. "She's certainly eating better than she was this morning."

Hannah had wondered at her mother's unexpected request to accompany her to Nathaniel's today, especially after Mama had quizzed her about the man so much the night before. But working alongside each other through the day had been thoroughly pleasant. Together, they'd given the small cabin a thorough cleaning, replaced the chinking in the two shorter walls, and put together a nice evening meal using food supplies they'd brought.

Misty M. Beller

In truth, it was like a pleasant day at home, working in tandem as they talked or hummed or just enjoyed the sounds of their diligence.

And after another day or two, she'd be done with the chinking and ready to start working the ground for a small garden plot. "Do you think Cathleen would mind giving up a few of her vegetable plants? I'd like to plant a small garden out beside the cabin, but it's too late to start from seeds, I think." She pointed toward the most level area in the clearing.

Her mother didn't answer right away, and Hannah glanced over her shoulder to see what she was doing. Mama regarded her with one of those all-knowing gazes. "Hannah, I doubt we'll be here all summer. I know your father wants to be home again before the first snow. Will Mr. Peak have time to tend the plants and harvest the produce? And store the food properly for winter? "

Hannah's chest squeezed. She wasn't ready to leave. How could she ride away from these people who had come to mean so much to her? Especially when they needed her.

The sound of a cow's moo outside saved her from having to manage an answer. What in the world? Hannah pushed to her feet and strode toward the door. Even though she wanted Itu's guardian to come visit the girl, they'd kept the door braced and her rifle propped beside the entrance. She wanted visitors, but only on her terms.

A peek through the slit in the door showed Nathaniel's tall form atop his mare, working their way around the edge of his cattle toward the barn. He certainly knew how to sit a horse—and make her heart beat faster watching him. But why had he brought the stock in from the pasture where they'd have a lot more grass than in this scant yard?

Something about his jerky movement as he dismounted showed a different kind of emotion than she'd expected.

Anger?

"It's Nathaniel. He's brought the cows in." She pushed aside the brace and pulled open the door. "I'll be right back." Maybe she should do the proper thing and wait for him to come inside, but he probably needed help. And something wasn't right.

Chapter Fifteen

I left the cavalry to escape this pointless violence.

~ Nathaniel

annah closed the cabin door and hurried across the yard to the barn. When she stepped inside, Nathaniel had tied his mare and was loading cords of rope over his arm. His quick, efficient movements still held a tension that clenched a knot in her midsection.

"Nathaniel? What's wrong?" She stepped inside and moved toward him to scoop up the last of the rope from the pile on the ground. "What are you doing with this?"

"A cow's dead." He spoke the words without looking at her, his voice almost void of emotion. Almost. "I'm keeping the rest of the herd here where I can watch them. At least for tonight. Will you help me tie this rope around the tree line for a fence?"

As much cord as this was, it still wouldn't stretch all the way around the clearing, which meant they'd be corralling the cattle in tight. She wrinkled her nose but followed Nathaniel out of the barn.

Her mother came out of the house to help, and the three of them had the small herd contained within a few minutes.

"I need to go check the food." Her mother wiped debris from her hands as she turned toward the house.

Hannah could go with her, but too many questions burned in her mind. Maybe she could pry more details from Nathaniel's locked jaw while they unsaddled his horse.

With him working on one side, and her on the other, they made quick work of unfastening the mare's saddle. She reached for a cloth to wipe the lathered horse down while he hauled the heavy leather off the mare's back and plopped it on the bar where he usually kept it.

She'd been waiting for him to settle enough to talk, but he was working so quickly, they'd be heading inside before she raised her questions. So she started in, even though his back was turned as he fumbled with something on the saddle. "Was it wolves?"

He shook his head, and the tendons in his jaw flexed as he turned and grabbed another rag. He moved forward to brush the mare on the opposite side from where Hannah was working. "An Indian killed her." The words were terse, and again he didn't look at her as he spoke. His expression was just like that of her oldest brother when he was trying to keep his rage bottled inside.

"How do you know it was an Indian?" A helpless cow could have been killed by sickness or a cougar or any number of wild animals. Or, if Nathaniel had seen clear evidence of knife wounds caused by a human, the culprit could have been from any race.

He whirled away and reached for his rifle leaning against the barn wall. Except he didn't grip the gun. His hand closed around something propped beside the weapon.

An Indian arrow.

Goose flesh rose along her arms as she watched him bring the shaft to her. She reached for it, her eyes not missing the dried blood covering the pointed head. She shifted her gaze to the paint and feathers at the other end.

"I don't know these tribal markings. Do you?" She lifted her focus to Nathaniel.

"All I know is they cut out all the meat from the cow, then left this lying atop her like a calling card." The hard glint finally softened in his eyes, turning to a question. "I don't know why they would make it so obvious. Do you think it's a taunt? What have I done to anger them?"

Through the layers of emotion in his gaze, she saw something that made her heart ache. Hurt.

He was such a good man, doing his best to mind his own business and help an innocent girl who'd showed up in his barn. At great personal expense, for that matter. And the natives were repaying his kindness by attacking the thing most important to him.

She'd finished rubbing down her side of the horse, so she moved around to where Nathaniel was standing. His jaw had clenched again. In anger, sure, but she was pretty certain part of his ire was there to cover the deeper injuries this attack had wrought. Maybe Nathaniel didn't even know their depths yet.

She placed a hand on his arm. "I'll ask Reuben if he knows which tribe this arrow came from. It's possible someone resents us keeping Itu away from them. But that's just speculation on my part."

He scrubbed a hand through his hair and turned away, pulling her hand from his arm. "Maybe they know I was in the cavalry and came to punish me for my crimes. If so, they should take the whole herd." His words were mumbled, but she could still pick them out.

Lord, help him forgive himself. She didn't know what offenses he was talking about, but the Nathaniel she'd come to know wouldn't wound a rabbit if he didn't have to for survival. He certainly wouldn't hurt a person of his own free will. *Whatever his past, Lord, let him see that his future can be new and unmarred.*

Nathaniel gulped the last ground-laden swig of his second cup of coffee as he sat on his cabin stoop the next morning. Between checking on the cattle and staying close to the house for Itu, the night had been impossibly long. He wasn't sure he'd gotten even one hour of unbroken sleep.

Which meant he wouldn't be worth much today.

Hannah had promised to come again and tell him what Reuben thought of the arrow's origins. The man seemed to have an unusual knowledge of the Indians in this area. Lord willing, he'd be able to shed some light on what Nathaniel should do next.

He certainly couldn't keep the cattle penned in this little rope corral much longer. They were already pushing against the restraint, and they needed better grazing.

But he also couldn't afford to lose another hard-earned cow. He had to keep them close. Maybe when Hannah arrived to care for Itu, he could herd the animals to pasture for the day.

He gazed at the trail where she'd ride in, wishing his thoughts could summon her. But he wasn't so lucky.

By the time he finished his third cup of sludgy dark brew, a whinny from the trail signaled Hannah's arrival. A second rider rode beside her. Reuben.

Tension eased out of Nathaniel like a pent-up breath. Hannah always knew what he needed, even when he couldn't bring himself to ask.

He stood to greet the pair as they approached, lifting a hand in greeting when they reached him. His weary mind wouldn't summon any words.

Hannah reached him first, her gaze scanning his face with a critical eye. He probably looked as haggard as he felt. "Did something else happen?"

He shook his head. "All was quiet through the night. The cattle are raring to get out of that rope, though. I'll take them to pasture in a little while."

She still studied his face, and he wanted to turn away from her scrutiny, but he couldn't walk away yet. He had to know Reuben's thoughts on the arrow.

"Why don't you let Reuben take them to pasture while you sleep?" She spoke the words low, a suggestion for his ears alone. At least she was protecting a little of his pride.

But he shook his head again and turned to the other man. "See anything you recognize on that arrow?"

Reuben held the weapon in his hand and raised it for another perusal. "It's pretty plain. No decoration except for this strip of black paint. That makes it hard to pin down to any particular tribe. I'd say the shooter may be far from his people and didn't have access to much decoration." He raised his gaze to Nathaniel. "Which would be in line with a Hidatsa, since they're mostly plains Indians living farther east. But it could also match a couple dozen other tribes. It's impossible to say for sure. At least, as far as I know."

The strength seemed to leech out of Nathaniel's shoulders, and he didn't have the energy to square them again. "What do you recommend I do?"

Reuben's focus shifted up to the herd of cattle. "Do whatever you can to prove yourself a friend to them. I'm not sure how to do that while they won't show themselves." His gaze shifted back to Nathaniel. "Eventually, they *will* come out of hiding. That will be your chance."

Desperation welled in Nathaniel's chest. "What about my cattle? I can't lose another."

"What you're doing now is wise, but don't kill yourself in the process." Reuben gave him a pointed look.

Nathaniel eased out a breath. The other man's validation felt better than he should allow it to. "All right." He turned to Hannah. "Do you mind staying with Itu while I take the cattle to pasture for a few hours?"

"Of course." She was still watching him with that gaze of hers that saw too deeply inside him. "How is she?" The tenderness that swept over her face made him want to pull her close.

But he didn't.

"She's more alert. I think maybe her fever's lower, but I'm not good at telling for sure." Was there anything he was good at? He wasn't so sure anymore.

A smile bloomed over her pretty face. "Fine. We'll have a nice day together. Did she tell you she's learning some English words?"

He raised his brows. "Really? She didn't mention it."

Pretty pink warmth rose into her cheeks. "Well don't tell her I told you. I think she wants to surprise you."

Oh, this woman was sweeter than a peppermint stick. He could look at that smile for days. Years.

She turned and started toward the barn. "I'll saddle your horse while I put mine away. Reuben, you're going with him to cut hay, right?" She didn't wait for an answer, just kept marching away.

Nathaniel looked back at Reuben. "Is she always so bossy?"

A hint of a grin touched the other man's face. "Pretty sure she is."

Hannah kept up a steady monologue, sometimes shifting into song, as she worked on the chinking from inside the cabin. Itu was definitely feeling better, as she stayed awake for a couple hours straight in the morning. She was so weak still and didn't seem to want to try to stand using the chair to help her stay upright.

Hannah had helped her up to use the chamber pot, and the brief effort exhausted the girl. But at least she was healing, and she didn't seem too shocked at the missing left leg. In truth, Itu was such a sweet child, she didn't protest much.

Either she really believed they were doing their best to help her, or she'd given up on her fate. Hannah could only pray it was the former.

While the girl slept that afternoon, Hannah worked on the outside chinking. She was determined to finish this wall today. The sky hung gray, and she sent up a prayer that the Lord would hold off any rain. The last thing she wanted was for her hard work to be washed away before the mud had a chance to properly cure.

As she worked, she gradually became aware of the quiet around her. Animal sounds had ceased in the woods. The silence made her skin tingle. Someone was watching again. The same person who'd killed Nathaniel's cow? Possibly Itu's mother or father.

She had to attempt to talk with them. Befriend them. That's what Reuben had said to do, and he'd spent many winters with his Crow friends before he married Cathleen.

Wiping the mud from her hands as best she could, she reached for her rifle and headed toward the woods. She would appear friendlier if she wasn't carrying the gun, but so much could happen in approaching an unknown Indian. She'd be foolish not to bring protection.

"Hello." She kept moving as she called toward the trees, making her voice as pleasant as she could.

No answering voice sounded, but she hadn't expected a response. It would be nice if the Indians would step from the trees before she reached them, but no buckskin-clad figure appeared.

"Do you want to see Itu?" Even if the person didn't understand English, maybe they would recognize the girl's name. "I can take you to her."

She'd reached the first trees bordering the clearing's edge, and she slowed her step to better see around each trunk. "I come in peace." What other words might an Indian know?

Her visibility into the shadowed woods was a little better now that she was moving into them, but the skin along her neck tingled the farther she went. Because someone was watching her? Or was it merely because of her own awareness of the danger she was venturing into?

As the trees thickened, a patch of pressed ground caught her notice. The area was behind a tree with a wide trunk, perfect to hide a person. Stepping toward the spot,

164

she glanced back toward the cabin, which was in perfect view. The dried leaves in the patch were crushed into tiny fragments, and a spot of barren dirt held imprints—possibly like that made from leather moccasins. She couldn't find any defined marks like what would be made by a boot heel or two.

Straightening, she scanned the trees deeper in the forest. Whoever had been here was probably still nearby. Watching her.

"Please show yourself. I only want to speak with you." Her voice held more pleading than she'd meant for it to contain, but this was getting ridiculous. She only wanted to invite the person in. Why all the secrecy? Even though she held a gun, she could hardly be a threat to an Indian brave.

"Please." She tried a final time. "I mean no harm. I can take you to the girl, Itu. She would be pleased to see you."

Her heartbeat thumped in her ears as she waited, holding her breath so she didn't miss a sound.

Nothing.

Letting out her pent-up air, she turned back toward the cabin. She'd tried. There was nothing more she could do until the stranger chose to show himself.

But as she stepped from the woods, she couldn't help walking a little faster, and even peeking once over her shoulder.

Someone was back there. Watching. Whether they meant harm or not was yet to be seen.

165

Chapter Sixteen

This…is what I've longed for. Even better than my dreams.

~ Hannah

athaniel couldn't get Hannah's story out of his mind. Whatever had possessed her to go into the woods to find the Indian who'd been watching the cabin? A woman alone facing one or more Indian braves would have little defense, even if she was carrying a rifle. Thank the Lord she'd not found them.

Now that dark had fallen, he might have a chance of sneaking up on the person, assuming they continued watching into the night. He could go to the barn to look in on Raven as he always did, then slip into the trees and move along the edge of the woods to the place she'd pointed out.

Standing in the corner of the cabin so Itu couldn't see him, he checked the bullets in his Colt pistol, then tucked the gun into the waistband of his trousers where he'd have easy access. His hunting knife hung in its normal spot at his side.

He moved to the girl and knelt by her side. "You're looking bright-eyed tonight. Did you enjoy your day with Hannah?"

The girl stared up at him with those huge, dark eyes, a hint of a curious smile touching her face. He'd not seen any sign she understood his words, despite the fact that Hannah had said she was learning English, but Itu didn't seem afraid of him. Even though he must look frightening, a big white man hovering over her.

Her acceptance of him was just one more thing that made his chest swell whenever he was near her.

He reached forward and tousled her hair with a light touch. A smile lit her face for real now, displaying something he'd never noticed before. Amongst the flash of her white teeth, a dark gap hid in the center of the top row.

"Aye, I see something different about you." He kept his tone light and playful, then tapped his own tooth that would mirror hers. "You're getting to be a big girl."

She snapped her mouth shut, but when he chucked her chin and grinned at her, a sheepish smile spread her lips wide again.

"You're cute as a new kitten." He ruffled her hair again, then pushed to his feet. "I'm going to the barn for a minute. I'll be back soon." And maybe he'd have a guest with him if he was able to catch the person watching the cabin.

He whistled as he strode to the barn, a lantern swinging from one hand. The stars were hidden behind a thick layer of clouds, and the air smelled of rain. Hannah had said she was worried a downpour would ruin the caulking she'd worked so hard on that day.

He still couldn't fathom how he'd been so lucky as to meet Hannah. Her family, too, for they'd all been a godsend to him.

A godsend. Had the Almighty actually led him to this place with these neighbors? But Hannah wasn't a permanent resident at Reuben's home. She'd mentioned several times that they were only here visiting.

He had to prepare himself for her to leave him. How he'd stop thinking about her constantly, he had no idea. She'd seared a place in his heart that made his chest ache even now as he thought about not seeing her again.

How far away did she live? She'd said they'd ridden about a month to get here. No short distance, to be sure. Yet maybe he could find a way to visit her, if he hired someone to watch his farm. After he had everything established.

And when would that be? Next year? He'd need to cut hay all summer to have enough for the herd he hoped to have by that winter. And traveling through the snowy months might be nearly impossible.

He'd have to let Hannah go. Put her out of his mind. Focus on the dreams he'd spent years working toward.

Raven greeted him with a nicker when he entered the barn. "Hey, girl." He stroked her neck, then rubbed the star on her forehead where she liked to be scratched. The mare bobbed her head, pushing into the pressure. "You like that, eh?"

With a final pat, he stepped back. "I'll be back in a minute."

He left the lantern on the packed dirt floor of the barn's aisle and opened the door only wide enough to slip through. He moved as soundlessly as he could toward the trees. His trousers were black and his shirt a dark brown, so hopefully he'd blend into the night.

Moving quietly through the trees was harder than he'd expected. He seemed to step on every dead leaf and stick in his path, and he forced himself to go slower so he could find better footing.

About halfway to the place where Hannah had seen traces of a person's presence, he paused to get his bearings. If the stranger stood there now, he might be able to see Nathaniel soon, which meant Nathaniel would need to be careful to creep soundlessly from tree to tree, hiding himself when he wasn't moving.

He started forward again, fading into every shadow he could find. Then he spotted the tree ahead, its wide trunk perfect to hide a person. He didn't see a figure stationed behind it, but he could be hiding on the other side.

Melting from tree to tree, he moved in a wide circle. It was impossible to keep his feet completely quiet among all the leaves and sticks, so he stayed far enough away that a person hiding behind the tree wouldn't be able to hear him. Hopefully.

But no one was there.

He circled completely around the tree but saw no shadows, no trace of a shadowy figure shifting away from him.

As he stepped from his hiding spot and moved toward the wide trunk, he eased out a breath. Should he be relieved he hadn't found the stranger? Probably not. He needed to deal with this lurker once and for all. Both for his own sanity and so he could put the cattle back out to pasture for good.

A sound made him freeze, and he caught his breath to listen for a repeat. There it was again.

The twitter of a bird.

Except what bird sang such a happy call during the pitch black of a cloudy night? That had to be a man. And it was probably the person he was looking for. A call meant there had to be more than one stranger.

He eased forward, shifting his gaze back and forth between his footing and the darkness ahead of him. Could he possibly sneak up on an Indian in the dead of night? He had no idea where the man was. His only guide were the twin bird calls, and he'd only clearly heard the second one.

Still, he had to try.

His heart thudded in his ears as he proceeded, shifting from tree to tree as he had before. But then a new thought slipped in. What if the Indian's call had been intended for him to hear and recognize. What if they were trying to draw him farther from the cabin so one of them could sneak in and grab Itu?

He stilled. She was alone and helpless. How had he been so blind?

Spinning, he charged back through the woods, ducking under branches and not caring a bit about how much noise he made. Let them hear him coming. The sooner he scared them off the better.

He burst into the clearing and slowed to catch his bearings. The cabin looked quiet. Shifting his direction toward the barn, he stopped long enough to grab the lantern, then jogged to the house, light in one hand and gun in the other.

Easing the door open, he scanned the room before he entered. Itu's face had softened in sleep, which must mean no one else was here. He scanned the area one more time, taking special care to peer into the corners and behind the door. No one.

He stepped inside and pushed the door closed behind him, his gaze seeking out the tiny body that barely raised the blankets on the bed pallet. He let out a long breath.

Itu was safe. He wouldn't leave her exposed to danger again.

All was quiet as Hannah rode into the clearing surrounding Nathaniel's cabin the next morning. Nevertheless, her muscles were balled in a knot.

Maybe she shouldn't have come alone. Her parents had both been reluctant. In fact, her father had asked her not to go. He'd already promised to help Reuben with the pipes he was boring to bring water into their kitchen. The older

Mrs. Scott had taken ill, keeping Cathleen extra busy, so Mama felt like she needed to stay and help.

Hannah could still see the disappointment in her father's eyes. Was she being so defiant he regretted ever accepting her into his life? When she was born, he'd given her his name and promised to love her, even though she was the child of Mama's first husband. The last thing she wanted to do was make him regret his choice.

Yet Nathaniel needed her. Itu needed her. The girl had staked her place in Hannah's heart from that first day when she was scared and shivering in the barn. And Nathaniel, well…he'd become so much more important to her than she'd ever expected. She wanted to help him, to be there with him. To be the woman she saw in his eyes when he looked at her.

And it didn't hurt that he was breathtakingly handsome.

The cattle lowed in their rope corral as she dismounted, but otherwise the yard was quiet. She should check in the cabin to make sure all was well before she unsaddled Sterling.

After tying the gelding, she stepped to the door. The hum of Nathaniel's deep voice drifted from inside. She knocked, and his "Come in," sent a warmth through her chest. She pulled the latch string and pushed the door open, then stepped in and blinked to adjust her eyes to the dimmer light.

"Thatta girl. You're doing it."

His voice drew her gaze to the open area where Nathaniel stood beside Itu. He was supporting her injured side, but the girl was standing and had a straight stick propped under her shoulder.

Itu shifted the pole forward, then her face twisted in a grimace as she leaned her weight on the wood and hopped forward with her good leg.

Hannah couldn't help a squeal as she clapped her hands and stepped toward the pair. "Well done."

Itu looked up at her with such a radiant smile, Hannah's chest tightened almost to bursting. She moved alongside the girl, wrapping an arm around her little waist in a hug.

Her hand brushed Nathaniel's side, and she looked up to see if she'd offended him with the touch. A grin stretched across his face, and his eyes twinkled as their gazes locked. He was as proud of the child's efforts as she was. And he'd gone through the work of crafting the walking stick.

Standing there with him, celebrating the joy of the moment and this sweet girl's first steps, the feeling of family settled over her with a rightness that swelled a longing in her heart.

Nathaniel broke eye contact first, dipping his head to look at the girl. "Another step?"

The child seemed to understand him, for she nodded. But her eyes showed fatigue. They needed to be careful not to overtire her.

"How about if you walk back to the blankets?" Hannah kept her voice cheery, but glanced at Nathaniel to make sure he caught her meaning.

He nodded. "Let's turn you first."

Hannah stepped away to allow them to maneuver. She couldn't help a smile at the way Itu's face scrunched in concentration as she shifted the walking stick, then stepped forward with her good leg.

The effort was hard, Hannah had no doubt. But with practice each day, Itu would regain her strength and find new balance. Soon enough, she'd be hobbling all around the cabin.

When Nathaniel laid the girl down, Hannah arranged the blankets, then stroked Itu's hair away from her tired face. "After I put my horse away, I'll come back to change your bandage." It wasn't a very pleasant job, so she made sure she handled the task first thing when she arrived each day.

Itu's eyes drifted shut, and Hannah quietly stood and turned toward the door. As she pulled it open, Nathaniel stepped up behind her.

"I'll help you get him settled." He didn't meet her gaze, just strolled along beside her, his eyes drifting toward his restless cattle.

Was he coming to give the girl quiet to rest? Or could he possibly want to spend time with Hannah? Or…maybe he just had work to do in the barn.

She had to stop reading what she wanted to find in each of his looks and actions. Nathaniel Peak was a gentleman, not a man in love.

It was her own heart that was leaning dangerously near that state. She'd do best to stop herself now before her eventual departure inflicted more pain on herself than she would already endure.

She searched for something to say to shift her mind onto a safer topic. "Are you going to cut more hay today?" Hay and cattle would be nice, businessy subjects.

He turned his gaze to her and nodded. "If that's all right. If you'd rather I stay close, though, I can."

She stole a look at him, but he was so near, walking right beside her, she couldn't hold his focus. "I'd always like to have you near, but I know you have a lot to do. I can take care of things here while you do what's important."

He stopped walking, and she did the same, raising her brows in question. His gaze had turned intense. "What's important is right here."

She could barely breathe with the strength of his nearness. His intensity. His words. *Right here.* Did he mean the cabin? The girl lying inside? Could he possibly mean her?

Nathaniel's hand cupped her cheek, and the warmth of his touch, the calloused, work-worn strength of him, made her lean in. For just a second, she let her eyes drift shut.

But then she forced them open. She had to know what he was thinking. To see his thoughts in his gaze.

And those eyes. He was nearer than before. His chocolate gaze had darkened to a rich coffee. His focus dropped to her lips, sending a tingle all the way down her spine. With everything in her, she wanted his kiss. To satisfy the craving his gaze had started.

His focus lifted back to her eyes, and he must have seen her longing. "Hannah." Her name came out as a breathy groan. He lowered his face until his breath warmed her skin, then he hovered there, almost as if he were warring within himself.

She reached up to slip her fingers around his neck. To pull him closer and clinch the decision for him. The silky texture of his hair as her fingers wove through caught her off guard, and she slid her hand farther up his head, relishing the thickness. The delicious feel of him.

Nathaniel groaned, bringing her focus back fully to his eyes. Those smoldering eyes. Then they blurred as he lowered his mouth to hers.

His lips weren't at all what she expected. Warm and gentle, yet with a strength that caressed her mouth, creating a longing deep in her core. She slid her fingers through his hair, around his neck, her hands seeking more of him.

His own hands slid over her back, down to her waist, holding her tight to him. She moved closer, craving his nearness. Wanting more of this man.

Then the strength of his kisses gentled, as though he were reining himself in. But it only intensified the longing inside her, creating an ache she could barely contain.

He groaned again, pulling his mouth away from hers. But he didn't go far, just rested his forehead on hers as their breathing mingled. "Hannah." This time his voice was hoarse, rich with the same longing that nearly strangled her insides. "I never thought to find a woman like you."

His hands moved back to her face, cupping her jaw, cradling her in his warm hold.

For a long moment, they stood like that, and Hannah worked to bring her breathing under control.

At last, he raised his head from hers, putting enough space between them that she could study his eyes. He ran his hands down the length of her arms, took her hands, and lifted them to his chest.

He studied her, making her wonder what he saw on her face. Did it please him? At last, he spoke. "I probably shouldn't have done that." His words made her stomach tighten. But his thumbs stroked the back of her hands, and his eyes grew earnest. "But I can't bring myself to regret it."

Her mouth tugged in a wobbly smile. "Me either."

His own face spread in a grin that sent a shiver of joy down her shoulders. He raised one of her hands to kiss the fingers, then lowered it again, releasing his hold. "I suppose we'd better take care of that horse."

He wove the fingers of his other hand through hers, holding them close to his side as he turned and reached for Sterling's reins. The horse had stood quietly beside them the whole time, good fella that he was.

And as they strolled the final distance to the barn, Nathaniel cradling her hand tight within the safety of his own, she sank into the rightness of the moment.

Yet even in the midst of her joy, she couldn't help the longing for more that tightened her chest.

Chapter Seventeen

The strength of this thing growing inside me is impossible to deny.

~ Nathaniel

The song swirling in her mind wouldn't be held back, so Hannah hummed as she filled the empty cracks on the cabin's back wall. The rain the night before had been light enough that the overhang of the roof had kept the mud mostly dry.

She smoothed out the final patch of new chinking, then stepped back to see if she'd missed anything. A job well done, as far as she could see now. She could always do a little more later if she found more cracks as the chinking dried.

For now, she'd best check on Itu and change the poultice on the stump of her amputated leg. When Hannah had replaced the bandage that morning, the wound looked raw and inflamed—not a good sign with the infection they were already fighting. And Itu's fever had spiked again. Hopefully the garlic poultice and the willow tea were helping.

After dipping her hands in the bucket of water she'd been mixing into the mud, she wiped her icy fingers on her skirt and headed around the side of the house.

She'd left the cabin door open to let in fresh air and a bit of sunshine while Itu slept, and also because it would allow her to hear if the girl cried out. As she stepped inside, she squinted against the dim interior and moved toward Itu's bed pallet. The soft snores that had been drifting from the child all morning had silenced.

"Are you awake, sweet one?" She kept her voice quiet in case the girl *was* still sleeping. She still couldn't see anything but bright circles as her eyes struggled to adjust to the darkness.

She knelt beside the blankets, and finally her vision cleared a little. Not enough though, because all she saw was a wad of covers. "Itu?" She touched the place where the girl's head should be.

Her hand pressed only a flat blanket. Unease churned in her chest. "Itu?"

She could see clearly now, but ran her hands over the length of the blankets just in case she was missing something. Where could the girl have gone?

Spinning, she searched the hearth, expecting to find her up by the water bucket. Now that Itu had tasted freedom with the walking stick that morning, she was probably trying to care for some of her own needs. That meant she must be feeling better.

Hannah pushed to her feet and scanned the room. *No Itu.* She must have missed her tucked into a corner, so she searched again, moving to the table to see if the girl was hiding behind it.

The child wasn't here.

She lunged for the door. Maybe Itu had gone to the barn. But even as Hannah's mind searched for rational places where the girl could be, her gut knotted in a hard ball. As weak and injured as she was, Itu could never have come all the way out here.

Someone had crept into the house and taken her.

But Hannah had to make sure she wasn't in the barn. Had to exhaust all other options, just in case.

The barn interior was even dimmer than the house, but she made sure to peer into every dark corner of every stall.

No frightened Indian girl huddling against the wall.

She whirled and marched out of the barn, then paused to scan the yard. "Itu!" She stood perfectly still to hear even the smallest whimper.

No sounds. Nothing except the chirp of a bird in the trees.

She could no longer deny the truth. Someone had stolen that sweet girl away. *Dear, God, show me what to do.*

Perhaps it was her parents who'd taken her, and they had every right to their child. But with the fever spiking again and the stump red and inflamed, the girl needed medicines urgently to keep the infection at bay.

She had to find them before they got too far away. Maybe she could take some garlic and willow bark with her. If she couldn't convince the parents to bring the child back to

Nathaniel's cabin, at least she could show them how to care for her.

Lifting her skirts, she charged back to the house. Inside, she grabbed the sack she'd used to bring over foodstuffs and piled all the satchels of herbals they'd been using for the girl. Garlic cloves. Willow bark. Astragalus root. Dried arnica and marigold petals. All the herbs and plants her parents nurtured so carefully for their medicinal stores.

Itu would need every one.

With the loaded sack in her hands, Hannah stepped out of the cabin and paused to take in the landscape. *Lord, show me how to find them.*

Her gaze dropped to the ground. Last night's rain hadn't created much mud, but it had softened the soil. Maybe she could find prints that would lead her in the right direction.

She started toward the tree where she'd seen signs of a person before. The grass had been eaten short and cattle hooves pressed deep in the ground where Nathaniel had the rope corral before he'd moved it a couple days before. That should make it easy to see fresh human tracks, especially with the softened ground.

But as she entered the woods, she saw no sign of fresh prints, especially those left by a man. The leaves around the trees didn't appear disturbed either. With the under layers of leaves still damp, it should have been easy to see anything amiss.

But nothing. She walked through the woods for several minutes and saw no sign of anyone.

Finally, she paused and scanned the area, working to press down her fear for the girl. "Lord, where are they? Show me." She focused on listening for the quiet voice inside her. It was so easy for her churning mind to override the Lord's guiding, but she couldn't let that happen now.

She started walking back toward the cabin. Since this direction hadn't been right, she'd need to look in other places. She kept her eyes scanning around her but focused most of her attention on listening for the Father's direction.

Back in the clearing, she turned right. If she followed the tree line around the area, she should find prints left by anyone escaping to the woods. The plan felt like a good one.

When she passed by the barn, she saw the impressions of boot heels in the dirt, but the indentations where water had run through the prints made it clear the marks were left before last night's rain.

So she kept walking. *Show me, Lord.* Her heart kept up a steady prayer with every step.

She'd made it almost full-circle around the clearing before she found what she was looking for. Among the deep ruts left by wandering cattle, the flattened sole of a leather moccasin was barely visible. She wouldn't have noticed if she hadn't been searching the ground so thoroughly.

As she examined the print with all the expertise her wilderness family had taught her, she noticed the buckskin stitching around the edges. Also, she noted the way the man pressed harder in his heel than most Indians who took effort to land on the ball of their foot.

Either this man wasn't an Indian or he hadn't been trained properly in the art of walking silently. Or perhaps he'd been carrying a heavy load that shifted his center of balance.

A load like an injured child.

She moved toward the woods, finding a couple more human tracks among the hoof prints. Once the man had moved into the thicker part of the trees, he'd turned south. His tracks here were easier to follow, as though he wasn't taking time to hide them. As though speed had been more important to him than stealth.

Maybe she should go back and find Nathaniel. But if she moved quickly, she could catch them right away and either hand over the herbs or take charge of the girl.

If she lost their trail, it would likely be impossible to find again.

And she had to find them. Itu needed her. This child's life depended on her.

Nathaniel herded the cattle into the rope corral as weariness weighed his bones. Moving the animals back and forth to pasture every day—at least half an hour's ride each way— was wearing on them all, but he couldn't take a chance on losing more stock to a hungry Indian.

But soon he'd see Hannah again. And that thought was enough to bring a grin to his face as it had all day. Swinging a scythe and moving hay that afternoon had given him plenty of time to think. He couldn't deny how much he'd fallen for this woman. Her kindness, her beauty, the way she made him want to be a better man—all of these had woven together into something that was a lot more than attraction. It seemed too new to call this feeling love, but one thing he knew for certain—he didn't want to let her go.

The problem was, he wasn't ready for her. His cabin was still unfit for any decent woman. He didn't have enough stock to make a real living, so he'd be existing meagerly off his savings for another year or so.

He simply didn't have a life ready for her. By next spring, things would be better. He'd have a lot of work done on the cabin and outbuildings. He'd have more stock. They wouldn't have proceeds from the sale of any cattle yet, but if she wouldn't mind growing and hunting for most of their food for another year or so, they should be able to manage well enough. It wouldn't be a well-to-do life, not like she deserved. But he wasn't sure he could ask her to wait *two* years.

She'd go back home with her parents, surely, and he could only pray she'd wait for him until he could come to her in the spring. It'd be hard to leave his farm for a couple months when he should be nurturing cattle and cutting hay and putting in a garden, but he'd do whatever he had to for Hannah.

He unsaddled Raven in the barn, then dipped his hands in a bucket of water and scrubbed his filthy paws, then his face. He had to dry himself with his dirty sleeve, so the effort might have only made things worse.

As much as he wanted to ask Hannah tonight, he should probably wait until he'd had a bath and a shave.

Tomorrow. If he could find the right moment alone with her, he'd ask.

As he strode toward the house, he couldn't seem to wipe the grin off his face. Maybe he could at least slip in another one of those kisses tonight. He'd kissed a woman or two before, but it had never brought him to life like having Hannah in his arms did. Her touch stirred him like nothing he'd ever felt.

When he reached the cabin, the door was cracked open. He rapped lightly to sound his presence, then pushed the barrier open. Inside seemed darker than usual, probably because the fire had died to only glowing coals. Hannah must have allowed the flame to fade when the room was too warm, but it certainly didn't feel that way now.

Itu's bed pallet was empty, and a scan of the room showed no one inside. He even looked behind the door, but the place felt as empty as a deserted cave. Where would they be? This was the first time Hannah hadn't had a warm meal cooking when he stepped in the door. That certainly wasn't her responsibility, and he shouldn't let disappointment knot his hungry belly the way it was. He simply needed to make sure they were fine, and maybe join them for a few minutes before she had to head home. So where were they?

Hannah must have taken the girl outside for fresh air. His gaze wandered to where he'd left the walking stick propped in the corner.

Still there.

He spun on his heel and marched back outside. "Hannah?" Maybe they were behind the cabin, soaking in the last few rays of sunshine for the day.

But as he rounded the corner and saw the grassy area empty of people, worry tightened a rope around his chest. There was something back here, and he stepped closer to see a bucket of water and in it, a mixture of chinking mud. He pressed two fingers into the stuff, and they came away almost dry. It had been several hours since she'd last used the mud.

Maybe as long as it had been since she'd added wood to the fire.

His pulse sped up a few notches. Something wasn't right.

"Hannah!" He yelled her name as he marched back around the cabin and inside. Maybe he could find some clue as to where she'd gone. Her horse was still in the barn, so she couldn't have taken Itu back to Rueben's house. And unless someone was helping her carry the child, she couldn't have gone far.

He didn't have much in this little cabin, so it shouldn't be hard to figure out if anything was missing or out of place—except for the woman and girl he loved. They were missing, and he'd do whatever was necessary to get them back.

It took going through everything he owned to realize that the herbs for Itu were gone. The rifle Hannah always carried with her was missing, too. A fact that gave him a sliver of relief. The food she'd brought that morning had been dumped out on the floor near the hearth, and the sack was nowhere to be found.

If she'd planned to be gone several hours, wouldn't she have taken food with her? Maybe not the abundance she'd brought that morning, but at least something. Or maybe she'd packed some of the food and he didn't realize it.

He forced out a long breath to still his racing mind as he scrubbed a hand through his hair. The few things she'd taken didn't give him any clear idea of where she might be. He'd best get outside and see if he could find tracks that would signal which way she'd gone.

It took much longer than he had patience for, but he finally found a trail of female boot prints about Hannah's size leading around the perimeter of the clearing. He couldn't begin to imagine what she'd been doing, but as long as he could follow these, surely he could find her.

The tracks became harder to follow when he reached the place where he herded the cattle to and from pasture each day, and he had to crouch down to examine the ground until he found her tiny prints. She was such a light thing, she barely pressed into the ground. If it hadn't been for the rain the night before, she may not have left a mark at all. *Thank you, Lord, for the rain.*

He followed the tracks into the woods and called her name a few times, but there was no response. He needed a horse to move faster. And more ammunition, since he had no idea what they'd be up against. And supplies.

Spinning, he sprinted back toward the house, loaded up everything he could fit into this saddle bags—his shot bag with extra bullets, a thick handful of roasted meat, a blanket, his flint, and the few matches he had left.

Then he ran to the barn and saddled his confused horse. Should he saddle Hannah's gelding, too? It would be harder traveling quickly with two animals while still trying to follow her tracks. And his mare could carry the three of them back. If he had to, he'd walk and let the others ride.

Saddling up seemed to take forever, his fingers fumbling with straps that were as familiar to him as his own shirt. Finally, he had everything tightened down and climbed aboard his tired mount. "Let's go, girl. We've only got an hour of daylight left. We have to find them now."

Chapter Eighteen

God, is this Your plan? Because I can't see the good in it. Guide me.

~ Hannah

Nathaniel found Hannah's tracks again and followed them through the woods. He wanted to call out for her. But if she was in danger, kidnapped by a band of Indian braves, announcing his presence might thwart his attempt to rescue her.

As darkness closed around him, fear pressed harder, weighing his shoulders, making it harder to breathe. He should have brought a lantern so he could keep moving after daylight faded completely.

The trail seemed to be going almost straight southward. Maybe he should mark the last print he was sure he could see, then keep riding south through the dark on the chance he might find Hannah and Itu. He just couldn't leave them to fend for themselves through the night.

Lord, let this be the right trail. Lead me to them.

He could see the occasional glimmer of stars through the tree canopy, but the darkness around him merged into a thick fog. It was time to make a marker he could come back to if he didn't find them in the night.

There wasn't much he could use for a sign, so he tore a strip off the hem of his white undershirt. The material was more of a dirty grayish hue by now, but hopefully he'd still be able to find it tied to a low branch.

He did his best to memorize the area, then nudged Raven forward. Since he didn't have to watch for tracks now, he could push the horse faster. He'd always had an innate sense of direction, which helped in the cavalry. He sent up a litany of prayers as he rode. For God's guidance, for Hannah and Itu's safety, and that he wouldn't arrive too late.

If Hannah had been kidnapped, he could only imagine what the men were doing to her. He had no idea how many there were or even whether they were male or female. He'd seen a few moccasin prints along with Hannah's boot impressions, so he was pretty sure they were all on foot.

"Nathaniel." The voice was so soft, he almost missed it.

He jerked hard on the reins as he peered into the darkness. "Who's there?" Maybe the noise had been only his imagination.

But then a rustle sounded behind him. He spun in the saddle and reached for his rifle. A shadow shifted, and he aimed the gun.

"Nathaniel, it's me." Hannah's voice sent a flood of relief through him.

The night was so dark, he could barely see more than shadows on her face, and her dark clothing faded into the blackness completely. "Hannah?"

She was a dozen strides away, and when she finally passed under a patch of light, he could see her familiar outline.

He slipped from his horse and half-ran to her.

She flew into his arms, and the solid feel of her body was an infusion of strength to his weary muscles. She wasn't an apparition his mind conjured to soothe his wild fears.

"You're all right." He gripped her tightly, wrapping his arms around her back. She was so tiny, he could almost enfold her twice around. Or maybe he was simply holding her as close as his own skin. He couldn't bring himself to let her go.

At last, she wiggled in his arms, a sign she either wanted space or couldn't breathe. He loosened his hold, running his hands down her arms to grip her elbows. With her face turned up to him, he could see some of her features, but her eyes were deep pools of shadows.

"Itu. I still haven't found her." Hannah's desperate tone reignited the fear in his chest.

"You mean she's not with you? I thought you'd been taken together."

She shook her head. "I was outside chinking the cabin, and when I came back in, she was gone. I've been following their tracks for hours but I lost them in the dark." She clutched his arm. "We have to find her, Nathaniel. The infection's getting worse in her leg, and her fever was rising

192

all morning. I'm afraid if she doesn't have the herbs, her body won't be strong enough to fight it."

The thought of that tiny little girl being hauled through these woods, sick and in pain, made his gut ball up in the knot that had been forming for hours now. "We'll find her. Do you know how far ahead they are?"

"I'm not sure." Her face turned the direction they'd been traveling. "I keep thinking I'll find them any minute. But it's so dark. If they've stopped to sleep for the night, I might walk right into their camp without knowing. Or worse, I might walk past them."

She was right. If Itu's captors had stopped for the night just ahead, he and Hannah didn't dare move on until daylight. On the other hand, if the Indians kept traveling in the darkness, they could be miles ahead by morning.

What do we do, Lord? Prayer had seemed to roll of his tongue so easily these past few days, as though he really expected the Almighty to answer him. Would He? Nathaniel had never interacted with the Lord on such a personal level, although he'd seen his mother do it. And he'd seen Hannah lift up casual prayers as she cared for Itu, as though in a continual conversation with God. Watching her had piqued his interest, and with his desperate need this night, he could only hope God might be listening.

"I think we should wait until daylight." Hannah's quiet voice held a pensive tone. "Moving forward tonight doesn't feel right."

Was this God directing her or simply an instinct? He had to ask. "Why doesn't it feel right? What inside you is telling you this?" His words didn't come out quite the way he meant them, but hopefully she would understand.

Hannah looked up at him again and didn't answer right away. Maybe he should try asking his question differently. As he replayed what he'd said, she might take it as an insult.

But she spoke before he could figure out what to say. "I don't have a peace about it. Every time I think of moving forward, my chest tightens and my hands get clammy. Not like fear, but... I can't explain it."

He struggled to make sense of her words. "So it's a gut instinct?"

"When my spirit has this much unrest, it's usually God guiding me a different way."

He let out a long breath as her statement sank in. "All right, then. We'll wait 'til first light."

Hannah awoke with her nerves pulled tight, her eyes springing open. It took a moment to remember why.

Itu.

She sprung upright, knocking the blanket aside. A groan beside her made her spin.

Nathaniel lay a few feet away, his arm covering his eyes against the light.

A rush of warmth softened the tension in her chest. He looked so...manly, sprawled out like that, yet his ruffled hair gave hint of the boy he'd once been. Her body craved to crawl over to him and fold herself in his arms. To enjoy the strength of his hold around her.

But not only would that be horribly improper, they didn't have time. The woods were already lightening, and the Indians had likely started on their journey again.

She leaned toward him. "Nathaniel, we need to get going."

He moved his arm from his eyes and looked at her. It took only a second for his gaze to register understanding. He lurched upright in a smooth motion. "There's some jerked meat in that saddle bag. Eat up while I saddle Raven."

His urgency cleared the remaining traces of sleep from her, and she quickly rolled up the blanket he'd let her use, then found the meat and pulled out a few pieces for each of them. Lord willing, they'd eat the remainder at midday on their way back to the cabin—with Itu.

Within minutes they were mounted, with her nestled in front of Nathaniel. She would watch for tracks while he guided the horse. Lord willing, they could move a lot faster this way.

The prints she'd followed the day before belonged to a single moccasin-shod man who carried a load. And the farther he'd progressed, the more tired he'd become, as was evident in the way he'd begun to drag his feet.

About a quarter hour into the ride, she spotted a flattened spot in the leaves, with enough tracks and churned leaves circling the area to make it clear this must be the place where Itu and her captor had spent the night.

"We were so close." Nathaniel's tone held an edge as she walked around the area, looking for more clues. He'd remained in the saddle so they could move quickly when she was ready.

She couldn't deny feeling the same frustration, but hopefully they would catch the man and girl soon. "How much of a lead do you think they have on us?" She wasn't as good with tracking time during the dawn hours.

"If they left the first moment they could see the ground in front of them, at least an hour, maybe more."

A reddish tinge caught her eye, and she bent down to inspect the ground covering. There was some kind of moisture on a dried leaf. A little darker than blood.

The knot in her belly pulled tighter, sending bile up to her throat. She'd seen this viscous substance before. The stump of Itu's amputated leg had oozed the first few days when they'd still been fighting high fevers.

She carried the leaf for Nathaniel to see. "Either he unwrapped the bandage on her leg, or the wound is oozing so badly it's leaking through the cloth." She had to press her lips together and breathe deeply to keep the images in her mind from churning up the meat she'd just eaten.

Nathaniel seemed to be doing the same. His gaze rose from the leaf to her. "Are you ready to ride?"

She nodded, then placed her foot on his and used his hand to pull herself up into the saddle.

Settling back against him with his arm around her waist was the only comfort in this horrible day. She'd not even let herself imagine what her family must be thinking. How worried they must be.

Would her father try to track her? Was he even now following their trail? Or was he so disappointed in the choices she'd made—choices he'd warned against—that he was letting her find her way back on her own.

And Mama. She couldn't think of Mama worrying.

For now, she had to focus on the ground in front of them. The misplaced leaves and broken twigs. The occasional impression of a moccasin print.

These were the things that would lead them to Itu. And the sooner they found her, the sooner Hannah could start doctoring her with the herbs she'd brought. If they waited too long, the child might be too far gone.

But she couldn't let herself think that far ahead.

They would find her. They had to.

They'd been riding all morning. Nathaniel glanced at the sky again, and it looked as if the sun had moved a few more notches than when he'd looked just a short while before. The midday mark had passed them by an hour ago, and they still hadn't found Itu and her captor.

Through most of the morning, Hannah had explained every track and sign she'd seen. Her insights had been fascinating to hear, and it was unnerving how much better she was at seeing the signs than he was. But as the hours passed, her explanations sounded almost defensive.

He could tell she was as frustrated as he that they hadn't found the girl. But her tracking certainly wasn't the problem. If it weren't for her impressive skills, they'd have lost the trail hours before. Maybe even yesterday evening.

When they'd stopped to eat a few bites of jerky and let Raven rest for a minute, he'd slipped his hands down the length of Hannah's arms and locked his gaze with hers. "You know you don't have to prove to me that we're on the right path. Right?"

Her focus dipped.

He'd lowered his chin to see into her eyes again. "I mean it, Hannah. Your skills are better than those of any man I've met, even the Indian scouts who rode with us in the cavalry. It's not your fault we haven't found her." It was his own fool self's fault for sleeping so late that morning, but he didn't say that aloud.

Hannah had looked up at him then, her expressive brown eyes luminous with all the fears welling inside her. Her lips had parted, and it took everything inside him not to press his mouth to hers. But she didn't need his advances just now, she needed comfort. And reassurance.

So he'd taken her in his arms and held her. And that had been almost as good as a kiss.

Now, he could feel both of their renewed energy starting to wane. If they turned back now, they'd reach his cabin sometime after dark. He had to get her back to

Reuben's place, though. There was no telling what her family thought about their overnight absence.

He'd sullied her reputation, no doubt. Maybe no one besides her family and Reuben's would know, but they would surely assume the worst of him.

If Nathaniel had a daughter who'd gone to visit the home of an unmarried man, then didn't come back for over a day, he'd be out of his mind with worry. In fact, he'd have gone to find that daughter and wouldn't have stopped until he'd been assured of her safety. And if there was any sign of her virtue being compromised, there would be the worst possible consequences to pay.

He had to get Hannah back. Her family may never approve of him as a suitor after this, but at least he could stop their worry.

Locking his jaw to hold that thought in place, he reined Raven to a stop.

Chapter Nineteen

This may well be the hardest battle I've ever fought.

~ Nathaniel

Nathaniel tensed as Hannah turned in the saddle to look at him, her eyes only inches from his. Her breath brushed his face, and it was everything he could do not to lower his mouth to hers. *Oh, God. You've got to help me here.*

"What is it?" Her words pulled his focus back to the reason he'd stopped.

He forced his gaze away from her, looking off into the woods ahead of them. This would be easier if he didn't have to stare into her pleading eyes. "We need to turn back. Your family's probably worried sick. I can't keep you out here any longer."

She gripped his arm, her hold tight enough to slow his blood flow. "No." The word bit the air hard. "We can't abandon her, Nathaniel. She'll die if she doesn't get these herbs soon."

His eyes moved to her face against his bidding. "She's not ours to worry over. She was given to us for a season, to help her through the worst of her injury. Now, I can only hope she's going back to her people who can help her. *You are my most important focus at this point.*"

"Nathaniel." Her pleading gaze drilled all the way to his core. "I can't leave her to die. What if they're just ahead? What if we find them in the next few minutes? I don't think I could forgive myself if we give up."

The frustration building inside him was almost too much to contain. What was the right answer here? As special as Itu had become to him, Hannah was everything. Her safety and happiness were of utmost importance. But those two qualities appeared to be at odds just now. One of them would have to be sacrificed for the other.

Was there a compromise? Maybe...if he could pull it off.

"How about if I keep going on foot. I'll take the herbs with me, and I won't come back until I find them and do everything I can for Itu. You take my horse back and let your family know what's happened." They may still come after him with a lynch mob, but at least the child would be helped before he breathed his last.

And Hannah would be safe.

"I won't do it." She shook her head with force. "I'm going after Itu whether you go with me or not. In fact..." Her eyes narrowed on him. "...you go back and tell my parents where I am. I'll keep going on foot."

Had she lost her mind completely? He held in a growl. "You're not going on without me. We've already determined this is likely an Indian brave who's taken her. What kind of man would I be to let you face him alone?"

Her eyes softened, and she raised her hand to cup his cheek. "Less than the man I know you to be."

Her quiet words, combined with the power of her touch, were a punch to his gut. He had to struggle to pull air into his lungs.

And still, they hadn't made a decision. If there was one thing he wanted between them, it was honesty—and of course, love, mutual respect, and this physical attraction that threatened to send him up in flames. But *honesty* was what he needed to focus on just now.

He met her earnest gaze, doing his best not to drown in her. "So what do we do, Hannah? What's the answer here? I'm not willing to disregard your safety, your virtue, or your family's concerns. But what you want also matters a great deal to me."

If anything, her gaze grew more intense. "Nathaniel, throughout my life, I've wanted to make a difference in the world. And holed up in that cabin in the remote Canadian mountains, I've never been able to help more than my own family.

"Now is my chance. Maybe I'm not saving the entire world, but I can help that little Indian girl. A child who's come to mean as much to me as any of my brothers or cousins. I can't let her go, Nathaniel. Everything in me says that if I turn my back on her, I'll be throwing away the work God's called me to. I can't do that."

A knot had been growing in his throat as she spoke, and he tried to swallow it down. This woman was more special than he'd imagined. How could he say anything to refute her spirit? The essence that made her so extraordinary?

"All right. I'll be with you every step of the way. But...one question?"

A tiny smile tugged at the corners of her mouth. "Yes?"

"Will your family hunt me down to string me up? Or will they wait until I bring you back?"

She leaned forward and pressed a kiss to his lips, a touch gentle enough to start his blood boiling just as she pulled away. Now the smile reached her eyes. "They won't be angry with you, just disappointed in me. I'll deal with it when the time comes."

He caught her face and pulled her back for another kiss. Not long, just a delicious tasting. Then he held her gaze. "We'll handle it together. Come what may."

Her shoulders relaxed as she let out a long breath, then nodded. "Let's get moving then."

Hannah's stomach had long passed empty by the time evening fell. Nathaniel must have heard the rumbling in her midsection, for he reached into his pack and pulled out a strip of jerky while the mare kept up a steady walk.

She glanced over her shoulder at him. "Is this the last of it?" He'd doled out their midday portions, but she'd seen how little meat was left that morning. She wouldn't put it past him to give her what was left and skip the meal himself.

He kept his eyes on the trail as he spoke. "I need to hunt, but I'm afraid if I use the rifle, I'll alert the man to our presence."

Itu's captor may already have known where they were, which was probably why they hadn't found him yet, but Nathaniel was wise not to make noise. If they found a decent-sized stream with fish, she could snag one or two for a meal. Or if they had enough time and some twine, she could set a snare. But that would require staying in one place longer than just the nighttime hours.

What else could she do to find a meal for them? This mountainous terrain didn't have much more than trees and rocks.

And birds. Maybe they could bring down one or two with a well-aimed stone.

"Nathaniel. If we were able to get a couple of birds, would it be safe to build a fire to cook them?"

He was quiet for a long moment, and she almost turned again to read his thoughts. But at last he spoke. "It's risky. How would we catch the birds?"

She glanced around at how the dusky light made the lanky lodge-tree pines look like a glaring army. Had she even heard a fowl in the past half hour? They'd have better chances during the midday hours. She exhaled a breath. *Lord, bring us food. Or show me what we should do.*

If they had to, this strip of jerky would suffice for their evening meal. Maybe in morning's light, she could find berries or something else to hold them over. She divided the meat in half and handed a piece to him.

"Eat it, Hannah." His deep voice rumbled in her ear, making her want to settle deeper into his hold. The more time she spent with this man, the deeper her love for him grew.

She turned her face so her cheek rested against his shoulder, her forehead leaning into the crook of his neck. "We both need sustenance. I'll only eat this half after you finish that piece."

The quick beat of his heart thumped in her ear. A steady drumming that eased her nerves. Helped calm the tempest in her chest. Together they would find Itu. They had to.

Lord, let us be in time.

Nathaniel barely slept that night. Not only because he wouldn't chance sleeping a moment past first light, but this night felt so much colder than the last. Probably because of the mountain they'd been steadily climbing all afternoon.

It wouldn't be right for him to share their only blanket with Hannah, not unless one of them was in danger of freezing to death. He'd already besmirched her reputation with this journey. He wouldn't put her in a position where their closeness might actually lead to impropriety. He loved her too much to chance anything between them, and he had his weaknesses just like every other man.

Especially where Hannah was concerned.

When there was just enough light to see his hand outstretched before him, Nathaniel rose and crept away as quietly as he could. Surely there were some kind of berries or edible plants on this tree-covered mountain. They needed something, or they'd have to hunt in earnest.

He hiked downhill for a good ten minutes and was just about to turn back when a patch of open land appeared through the trees. Maybe he'd find something edible there. One of the Indian scouts with the cavalry had shown him some plants and berries his people thrived on. He wasn't sure he could identify any of the plants by sight unless they had the same flowers blooming as he'd seen before, but the man's words about the berries had stuck in his mind.

The trees cleared away to form a small grassy patch with tall weeds and light blue flowers scattered around the area. He didn't recognize any as the plants the scout had shown him. Over on the far side, though...could those be chokecherries? It was hard to tell in the semi-darkness, but they were either chokecherries or black cherries, he'd bet his last dollar.

And either one sounded as good as a beefsteak just now.

He strode to the plant, which turned out to be several bushes growing close together. The berries had a reddish-tinge, which meant they were probably not quite ripe. But surely they were far enough along to eat, even if they were sour enough to pucker his cheeks.

He scratched a bit of bark off one of the branches and leaned closer to sniff. Definitely chokecherries. That unusual scent made them easy to distinguish.

Pulling a few berries off one of the clusters, he popped them in his mouth—the whole handful. If he was going to die of poison berries, he would die with a full stomach.

These wouldn't kill him, though. Maybe just give him a belly ache if he ate too many under-ripe ones.

He sucked in a breath as the juices from the tart fruit touched his tasters. *Woo-wee.* But his gut let out a hungry growl, so he loaded another fist-full in his mouth.

Now to bring some back for Hannah. He pulled out his shirt tail and filled the cloth with the darkest berries he could find. They should probably ration them throughout the day.

When he made it back to camp, Hannah was already up and had the blanket tied behind the saddle. She eyed him with wide eyes as he approached, holding up his laden shirt.

He couldn't help a grin. "I brought breakfast. And the noon meal, too. We'll need to make them last so we don't eat ourselves sick."

She stared at the mass of reddish black berries in his arms. "Cherries?"

"Chokecherries. Have some."

Those seemed to be the magic words, for she reached in and grasped a handful, then popped half of them into her mouth. Her way of eating was a little more graceful than his, but not too much. She was clearly as hungry as he'd been.

After gulping down several handfuls, she wiped her mouth with her hand. "Can we take them with us? We need to get going." She spun and retrieved the leather he'd had the jerky wrapped in.

They both moved quickly, and in a couple minutes had the berries stored and Raven saddled. He let her climb up first, trying not to notice her slender ankles as her skirts pulled during the mounting. One day she would be his, Lord willing, but he'd do best not to tempt himself before then.

This woman would be an enticement impossible to resist if he wasn't careful.

Chapter Twenty

Lord, where is Your plan in this?

~ Hannah

nother long day in the saddle, and they still hadn't caught up with Itu and her captor. It was as though the man knew they were there and stayed just out of their grasp.

They also hadn't found clean drinking water since midmorning. Now, halfway through the afternoon, Hannah's throat felt too dry to speak, and her eyes ached from watching the signs so closely. And maybe she'd missed the important clues. Maybe she'd lost all her skills when it came to tracking.

"I think he must know we're back here, and he's doing his level-best to stay a few steps ahead." Nathaniel must have been reading her thoughts. And his words soothed the raw edges from her guilt. His arm draped loosely around her helped too, as he pushed his mare into a faster walk down the grassy slope at the base of a mountain.

But even if her tracking skills weren't at fault, the fact remained that Itu was probably getting worse with every hour they couldn't reach her. Whoever had taken her was moving too fast to be giving her the care she needed. Hannah had seen traces of that bloody drainage again where the pair had slept for the night, and also in a couple other places where they must have stopped to rest.

"Where do you think he's taking her?" She scanned the ground a little farther ahead, her eyes picking out the trail the man had taken through the grass. Tracking in these conditions was much easier than in the woods they'd been traveling through.

"I don't know this country, but I suspect their people have a camp somewhere around here. I hope he's taking her to a place where she can get help."

It was the same thought she'd had more than once, and it clenched the knot in her middle just like it always did. "What will we do if we don't catch them before they reach the others?"

Surely the people in the camp wouldn't allow Nathaniel and her to ride in and help, just like that. Especially when they saw that part of the girl's leg was missing. What if the Indians didn't have the right remedies to help her?

"We'll just have to catch him." Nathaniel urged the mare into a trot as the ground leveled off into a valley. His arm around her tightened with the bouncy gait.

The man's trail turned south down the length of the valley, tracking between the two mountains rising high on either side. A stand of evergreen trees clustered in the distance, and as they neared, the sound of running water gurgled back to them.

Hannah sat up straighter. "I think there's a spring in those trees." Her mouth seemed to go dryer at the mere sound.

Nathaniel guided the mare into the copse of woods and up to edge of a creek, just downstream from a small pool of water. Hannah jumped to the ground and moved to the clean water near the spring.

The icy liquid tasted like heaven as it moistened her parched throat. She needed a bath more than she wanted to consider, but it would have to wait. For now, just splashing the cold water on her face was enough to stir her senses to life.

"Come feel this, Nathaniel. It's wonderful." She raised another handful of water to her face, spreading the refreshment down to her neck. How dirty was she exactly?

Nathaniel hadn't joined her yet, so she turned back to see what he was doing.

A hand clamped over her mouth. Another gripped around her middle, strapping her arms to her side.

She tried to scream. Tried to twist and see who was holding her. It couldn't be Nathaniel, not with this painful grip. The hand over her mouth smelled like horse droppings, and tasted even worse. Was this Itu's kidnapper?

Something flashed in front of her eyes, then a rawhide strap replaced the hand to gag her. It was jerked tight as someone tied it behind her. She fought to turn her head again, and finally succeeded as the vise holding her tight hauled her up.

She only caught a flash of several tawny figures before she was spun in the air, tossed like a sack of flour, then draped over a man's shoulder. His arm still pinned her hands to her side, so she had no leverage to struggle. Her middle burned with the pressure of her body bent in half, and the sour smell of bear grease stung her nose.

Hanging there upside down, she struggled to pick out the voices humming around her. All male, and none of the sounds made sense. These must be friends of the man who'd taken Itu. Did that mean they were near his camp?

Had he sent these people back to kill her and Nathaniel?

Oh, God. Where's Nathaniel? Don't let them hurt him.

She could only see the lower half of men's moccasined legs as they moved in a pack. Her stomach ached from trying to hold herself still so she didn't bump her captor. Every part of her revolted from his touch. What would they do to her? Would she have a chance to see Itu? To explain what the girl needed?

God, help me. Was it worth her virtue—maybe even her life—to keep the child from death? She had to believe it was. At this point, there was no turning back.

The men walked for what felt like an hour. None of them rode horses that she could see, but she heard the occasional snort of an animal nearby. Maybe that was Raven? Surely if they had Nathaniel similarly bound, they were bringing him along, too.

He had to be alive still. The alternative was too awful to consider.

At last, the sounds of other voices drifted around them. Women, and a few high-pitched shouts from what must be children. She craned her neck and caught a glance of buckskin-clad figures and long black braids. But the ache in her entire body made it hard to lift herself enough to see more than a glimpse.

The sunlight was suddenly cut off as they entered a dim area. A lodge of some kind. She couldn't see much on the ground, but then she was lifted high and flying through the air again.

She tensed as she landed on the hard ground with a thud that stole her breath. Her chest fought to draw air, and with the gag in her mouth, she could only breathe through her nose. She struggled onto her side, gasping as her body screamed for air.

A heavy moccasin struck her shoulder, pinning her to the ground. She could barely see, couldn't think except for her desperate need for breath.

Then blessed air finally crept into her chest. She took in another mind-cleansing dose.

She could finally look around now, but the sight just above her almost stole her breath again. A massive Indian brave towered over her. It took everything in her not to shrink away from him. She couldn't show these people her fear.

As least, not the full depths of terror threatening to spew up her throat.

Another brave appeared beside her, jerking her arms up to bind them. They were taking away her freedom, one leather strap at a time. At least her hands were being tied in front, so she could use them a little.

As soon as he finished and stepped away, she slid a glance sideways.

People strode in and out of the lodge, talking amongst themselves. Mostly men, but two women stood or knelt over something on the other side of the shelter. The people blocked her view of whatever they were working with.

Then one of the men pivoted and stepped away, giving her a clear view of a trouser clad leg. The same leg she'd ridden in front of for two days now.

Nathaniel.

He was lying so still, and she'd not heard a sound from him. Maybe he was gagged like she was. Maybe he wasn't moving so he could lull his captors into thinking he wouldn't fight them.

Surely they hadn't hurt him.

Lord, keep him safe. Both of us. Help me to find a way to help Itu. Please don't let this all be in vain.

Another Indian knelt by her feet, tossing up her skirts and tying her ankles tight together. Thankfully, her boots kept the leather from rubbing her skin the way the cords were rubbing her wrists.

She wanted to close her eyes tight and squeeze out the image of the braves standing guard around her. But she needed to keep her wits. Learn everything she could about these people so she could find a way to escape.

If they'd just take the gag off her mouth, she would try to tell these captors that she and Nathaniel had only come to help. And what of her bag of herbs? They'd been tied on the horse with the saddle bags. The Indians would surely go through their things. Would they recognize the importance of each satchel and bundle? *Lord, don't let these people toss the herbs in the fire.*

At last, the hubbub died down as most of the people left the tent. Only two braves remained, one sitting cross-legged near her feet and the other perched near Nathaniel. Guards, no doubt.

The lodge was almost barren except for a pile of furs stacked at the edge. Was this reserved as a holding area for prisoners? Did they really have captives so often that they needed to devote an entire tent for them?

And what exactly were they holding her and Nathaniel for? Would they receive a trial or at least be given a chance to speak? The longer she lay there, the more her mind churned with questions.

But that was better than wondering why Nathaniel still hadn't moved. The fact that his hands and ankles were bound had to be good. That must mean he was alive and the Indians expected him to wake. But why hadn't he? Even with an awful head injury, he should have awakened during the first hour. What could be wrong with him?

She couldn't seem to focus her thoughts into steady prayer, just frantic pleas to God. Maybe reciting Scripture would help. She started with Psalm 23, but she'd said it so many times throughout her life, she no longer had to think about the words. Her mind simply recited each verse by rote.

So she switched to one of her favorite scriptures in James about being thankful for trials because they produced a host of good character traits, especially stronger faith. That verse was as pertinent to her situation as she could find. *Lord, strengthen my faith through this. Surely You have a reason for bringing us this far only to be taken captive. Help me hear Your voice through every part of this ordeal.*

The longer she lay there, the more her stomach growled. Surely her guard heard every rumble. But every time she glanced at the man, he was looking over her head, or glancing at the fire ring in the center of the lodge. Never looking at her. Did they ever plan to feed her? She and Nathaniel had only eaten berries that day, and merely a few strips of venison jerky the day before. Given the opportunity, she could eat an entire deer by herself. But of course she'd share with Nathaniel.

The buckskin flap covering the lodge's entry jerked aside, and a man stepped in. He was tall and broad, more so than some of the other men. And his face held a fierceness worse than the darkest thundercloud.

For only a second, his gaze landed on Hannah, and it took everything in her not to shrink back from the intensity of his glare.

Could this be the man who had taken Itu? Who carried her on foot for two days, alluding them every step of the way?

He spoke to the man sitting by her feet, and the guard responded with a few quick syllables. The first man spouted off a long string, looking even more agitated than before. The Indian at her feet rose with a grunt, not looking much happier than the other brave.

He pulled a knife from the sheath at his waist and swung it down toward Hannah's feet. She had to bite her jaw not to yelp and jerk her legs backward, but she couldn't show weakness. She had to hold in her fear.

The blade hit the leather tie binding her ankles and sliced through the hide with barely a pause. A knife that sharp could pierce human flesh without a second's delay.

One step brought the man to her side, where he grabbed her arm and jerked her to her feet. Her legs had gone numb, and she tried to lock her knees to keep herself upright. He was pulling her forward, though, and she stumbled along as he mostly dragged her.

They followed the first man out the tent opening. She turned for a final look at Nathaniel to see if his eyes were open, but she couldn't see more than a quick glance. Yet that image seared itself in her mind. His face tight, his hands gathered in front of him, wrists tied. Nothing about him looked relaxed.

She knew the feeling exactly.

Her guard dragged her forward. and they passed several lodges of varying sizes, then wove between two onto another row of tipis. Finally, they turned toward one of the dwellings, and the man leading ducked inside. Her guard pushed her in next, his massive paw gripping her arm tight enough to stop the blood flow.

Inside, the place was dim and cloudy from smoke. A small fire sat in the middle, and several people moved about the area. Sobbing sounded to her left, drawing her focus to a woman sitting beside a pallet of furs.

Hannah was pushed that direction, and it only took a moment for her eyes to make out the image atop the hides.

Itu.

She dropped to her knees by the girl—with the help of a shove by her guard—and reached for the child's hand. "Itu, my love. How are you?"

The girl opened her eyes a tiny bit, and when she saw Hannah, her mouth curved into a small smile. Heat emanated from her hand, and Hannah reached to feel her cheek.

A voice sounded beside her, and the tone made her pause with her hand in mid-air. The woman who'd been sobbing was now looking at her with a stern brow, saying something. She looked to be around Hannah's age, or maybe a little older. Itu's mother?

She clearly wasn't happy with Hannah's nearness, but Itu murmured something in a weak voice, and the woman motioned for Hannah to continue.

Had she been brought to help at Itu's request then? That made sense, and it also eased a little of the pain in her heart. They still had much work to do to make the child better, but at least she would be allowed to help.

Tentatively, she reached again to feel the girl's face. Burning with fever, as she'd suspected. The infection must be spreading through her body. They needed to fight it with every herb she'd brought.

This girl's life still hung in the balance. And now Hannah and Nathaniel's fate looked just as precarious.

Chapter Twenty-One

So helpless. I hate this impotence.

~ Nathaniel

Hannah turned to the adults gathered around her. "Where is the satchel that was tied to the horse?"

Only blank looks answered her. Did none of them understand English?

She cupped her hands in front of her like she was holding a basket by its base. "My things?" What else could she do to make her request clear? She turned back to the girl. "Do you want a drink, Itu? I need my herbs to make a tea." She wasn't sure how much the child had picked up from watching her each day in the cabin, but maybe she would understand and help interpret.

One of the men spoke something, then turned from the group and moved to another part of the lodge. Too many people blocked her view of what he was doing, but when he returned with Nathaniel's saddle bags, she smiled. "Yes." He didn't have the satchel she'd tied on top, but maybe they'd stuffed it inside.

She reached for the pack and checked the contents of one side. Their blanket had been crammed inside, but everything else looked as she'd seen it last. She reached for the other flap. There, right on top, was the buckskin satchel she'd used to carry the herbs. *Thank you, Lord.*

Over the next few minutes and with many awkward hand motions to those around her, she managed to find and heat water over the fire to steep the teas.

Next, she needed to remove the girl's soiled bandage and make a poultice to begin drawing the infection out. From the haphazard appearance of the filthy cloth, it looked as if the bandage had already been removed and reapplied at least once. As she worked to pull off the old wrap, she tucked herself over her work to keep the others from seeing the amputated limb. Not only would the sight and smell be gruesome if the infection was as bad as she suspected, but she was a bit nervous they'd be angry at the way the child had been permanently maimed.

Not that she and Nathaniel had had a choice in the matter. It had been a choice of losing the leg or losing her life, and every sweet smile from the girl made it clear her life was of much greater importance.

As she pulled the wrap away, an angry voice sounded just behind her. The girl's mother, if Hannah wasn't mistaken.

She didn't acknowledge the words—not that she knew what the woman had said—just kept working to clean the stump. Although she couldn't help but stiffen her spine, preparation for the blow from behind she feared would come.

No one struck her, thanks be to God, and she kept working, applying the poultice and wrapping everything up in the soft buckskin someone had brought her. The cloth bandage would be much better, but she'd need to wash the old one before it could be used again.

By the time she finished, the tea was ready, and she scooted beside Itu's head to help her drink. "This will help you feel better." She brushed the girl's hair from her face, taking note of the coating of dirt that hadn't been there two days ago. Her hair needed a good brushing, too.

She took her time helping the child drink, humming and talking as she usually did. Stroking her hair and her arm, anything she could find to soothe. Itu seemed barely awake at times, and beads of sweat rolled down her brow.

Hannah tore a patch from her skirt's hem and soaked it in cool water to soothe the heat. Sometimes the teas appeared to make things worse just before they did their best work. *Lord, let that be the case now.*

Through everything, she couldn't stop the fear that nipped at her mind. *What of Nathaniel?*

Could she get Itu to ask for him, too? Did she have enough sway with these people to ask herself? Probably not.

If Nathaniel was hurt as badly as his unconscious state seemed to indicate, he needed to be here, too, where she could tend him. Her heart ached at the thought of him suffering alone in that lodge, only a stoic guard watching his pain.

She had to try.

As Itu seemed to settle into a doze, Hannah turned back to the man who'd been guarding her. She pointed in what she hoped was the direction of the lodge where they were holding Nathaniel. "Can you bring the man?" She held her hand up beside her, palm down, as though she were measuring someone taller than her. Then she crossed her wrists in front of her the way they'd been when her hands were bound. "Bring the man." She pointed to the ground beside Itu. "Here."

If they understood her, it may be a miracle. But something must have made sense, for the man looked to one of the others and spoke a string of sounds.

Their words volleyed back and forth several times, and finally the man who she was fairly certain was Itu's father bit out a harsh sound. The other brave turned to one of the youths near him and uttered a word. The lad turned and strode out of the tent. Was it too much to hope that he'd been sent to bring Nathaniel? If so, there sure had been a lot of discussion about it.

She sat quietly while she waited, either for Itu to awaken and need something, or for them to bring Nathaniel. She'd already set more tea to steep so she could have the girl drink when she awoke.

Itu's mother still sat nearby, at the child's head, and Hannah offered a friendly smile. The expression took effort through all her worries, but the other woman didn't even seem to notice. Her focus was locked on the girl, and her lips moved as though she were praying.

Hannah knew nothing of their religion. In fact, she wasn't quite certain which tribe these people were from. But prayer was her best option, too. *Oh, God, be with us.*

As she lifted up each of them to her Heavenly Father, the door flap on the lodge pulled aside, and the youth who'd left a few minutes before stepped in. Behind him came the most beautiful sight she'd seen in ages. "Nathaniel."

His hair and clothes were rumpled, and his jaw was locked in a hard line.

The man beside him—his guard from the other lodge—had a rough hold on Nathaniel's arm.

When he saw Hannah, his eyes ran over her, drinking her in. Maybe checking for injuries. For her part, she couldn't take her eyes off his handsome face. She patted the ground beside her, but of course he had no power to choose where he would sit.

His captor brought him to stand by Itu's feet, and Nathaniel's eyes flicked to the girl. "Is she...?" It wasn't hard to decipher the question he hated to ask.

"She's alive." She shifted her gaze to the girl's sweat-glistening face. "Fighting a great infection, but I've given her everything I brought—teas and a poultice. She seems to be resting now. I hope her body's strong enough to fight this."

She looked back up at Nathaniel. He must be exhausted, and he had injuries of his own. A glance at his guard showed a face so stern, she wasn't likely to get help there. Still, she pointed to Nathaniel, then patted the ground beside her. "He needs to sit."

"Don't worry about me, Hannah." Nathaniel's warning came just as the guard pushed Nathaniel into the spot with a downward shove. Nathaniel did well not to topple forward onto the sleeping girl, especially with his legs still bound. But he caught his balance and eased down to his knees.

She shouldn't focus too much attention on him, for she was pretty sure the Indians had only allowed them this much freedom so they could tend Itu. So she kept her head facing toward the girl as she spoke softly to Nathaniel. "Are you hurt?"

"No." His response was just as quiet.

"But you were unconscious for so long." The last thing she needed was for him to play the hero when he really had an injury she needed to treat.

"Only for a minute. Then I was feigning sleep to see what they would do. When they took you away, I could have kicked myself for the act."

She slid a glance at him, just enough to take in his features again and replenish the picture in her mind. She could never get enough of watching him. "I think Itu asked for us. That's why they brought us in here."

He shifted his focus to the girl. "I suppose that means I don't need to worry about getting us away from here any time soon?" His words were so soft she could barely make them out.

She followed his gaze. "I'm here to help her. I can't leave until God tells me different." But she couldn't help the dread that hung around her like a sodden quilt. What would her family do about her disappearance?

Nathaniel couldn't do much to help Hannah or Itu, especially not with his hands and legs still tied. And the helplessness chafed more with each quarter hour. Especially with the anxious lines tugging at the corners of Hannah's eyes the longer the day progressed.

How had he let them be taken off guard? Kidnapped and now held hostage against Itu's life. For he had no doubt that if Itu didn't pull through this fever, he and Hannah would not walk out of this camp alive. And he was fairly certain he wouldn't get Hannah to leave until she was sure the girl was out of danger.

Would the Indians allow them to walk away when the girl was well? Or would he have to sneak them out?

Night settled outside the lodge, and they were finally given a small meal of pemmican and roasted meat. Enough to keep them alive, but not as much as even the women around the campfire ate.

It was clear the people resented him and Hannah. With a few of them, the emotion seemed closer to seething hatred. Especially the man who Nathanial was fairly certain was Itu's father.

The woman who never left the girl's head appeared to be the mother, and her occasional cajoling seemed to be the only thing that calmed the man. Nathaniel didn't miss the way he watched Hannah, though. At times, his glare was so harsh, even from across the lodge, it was all Nathaniel could do to keep from confronting him.

Was this the stranger who'd been lurking around the cabin for so many days? The blackguard who'd killed his cow. The thought swelled fury in his chest, but he did his best to force it away.

For now.

They were given a single blanket to sleep with that night, and it appeared they were to stay by Itu's side. A handful of other Indians bedded down in the lodge, with the venomous father lying in front of the door. There would be no escape this night, even if they wanted to.

The night was colder than the past two they'd spent on the trail, even though they were now inside the lodge with a fire burning in the center.

"We should both sleep under this." Hannah unfolded the blanket, the rough wool kind he'd seen handed out at reservations. Were these people escaped from government land? That was certainly possible, as he'd chased down his fair share of runaway bands while in the cavalry. It was surprising none of these spoke English, though.

He nodded toward the group around them. "I suppose we have plenty of chaperones." Then he raised his bound wrists with what he hoped was a humorous tone. "And you certainly have nothing to worry about with me trussed up."

Her smile was so weary he almost couldn't find the lightness in it. "I don't ever worry about you."

She shifted beside him and spread the blanket over their legs, then pulled it up to their shoulders as he lay down. When she was settled, they both lay on their backs, at least a hand's breadth between them.

The steadiness of her breathing filled the air around them as he stared up into the darkness. How could she breathe so normally when his heart raced double-time and he had to push out each shallow exhale? Even lying in the midst of a strange Indian camp where they were despised and held captive, this woman affected him all the way to his core. And with their future so uncertain, everything within him wanted to tell her exactly how he felt. Maybe not the long-term plan, but at least he could speak of this burning ache in his chest.

"Hannah?" He kept his voice to a low whisper, just in case any of the others understood more English than they let on.

"Yes?"

"I'll do everything I can to keep you safe." He wanted so badly to promise he'd not let anything hurt her, but he knew too much about what happened when there was bad blood between Indians and whites.

The blanket shifted, and her hand covered his bound ones. "I know you will. With both you and God here, I'm not afraid."

Her trust raised a burn to his throat, and he fumbled to take her hand between his. "No matter what happens, I need you to know that I love you." He didn't breathe as his words settled between them.

Did she feel the same? He'd thought maybe she did, but this was probably too soon. She'd only known him a few weeks. How could she possibly develop such a deep sentiment? Especially if she'd lived as isolated a life as he suspected. She probably wanted to experience more before tying her affections to one man.

He, on the other hand, had spent more years experiencing life than he could stomach. He knew without a doubt she was the woman he'd been looking for all these years, both while in Virginia and traveling with the cavalry.

But now he'd spoken his feelings and put her on the spot. The last thing he wanted was to scare her away.

He scrambled for something to say to clarify things. "I don't mean that you have to feel the same way. I'm sure you probably don't. Not yet. I mean..." He was making a muddle of this. Inhaling a deep breath, he tried once more. "I just wanted to say it, in case anything... You know, in case I don't have a chance again."

"Oh, Nathaniel." She let out a sigh. That couldn't be good, could it? But then she scooted closer, and the weight of her head rested on his shoulder. "I hoped one day to feel this way about a man. It seems almost too good to be true."

Her words should fill him with satisfaction—and they did. But he couldn't help being sidetracked by the irony in her last statement. "Too good to be true that we're being held captive in an Indian camp?"

Her cheek nestled deeper into his shoulder. "I'd rather be held captive with you than free with anyone else."

He couldn't help a chuckle, despite their circumstances. "Me, too, Miss Grant. Me, too." He stroked his thumb over her hand that was still tucked between his. But the longer he pondered her words, the more reality sank over him.

God, I don't deserve this woman. Show me how to protect her. How to love her.

Chapter Twenty-Two

Lord, have You brought me to this place for such a time as this? Use me for Your plan.

~ Hannah

Hannah awoke to the sound of quiet crying.

She sat upright, turning to look at Itu in the faint light from the fading fire. The small figure still lay there, barely raising the thin blanket Hannah had pulled over her the last time she'd given her tea in the night. A figure knelt beside the girl, bent over. Keening. The crying must be coming from Itu's mother.

Had the girl passed in the night?

Hannah's stomach knotted as she scrambled toward them, slowed by her ankles that had been bound again. She wanted to ask if Itu still breathed, but the woman wouldn't understand her words, and speaking would only wake the others.

She reached the child and pressed a hand to her cheek. Heat still emanated from her skin, and steady, raspy breaths drifted through her lips. Much the same as when Hannah had seen her last.

So why was the Indian woman crying? Hannah turned to her, and even in the dim lighting, the sharp knife of grief was evident in her hunched rocking. The low sobs seemed to tear from her inmost being.

It was impossible to kneel there and watch the woman's distress without trying to help. Did she cry because she feared her daughter wouldn't survive this most recent bought of infection and fever? If Hannah felt that way, she would likely be sobbing, too. Itu was such a dear, loving girl. So brave, especially for one her age.

She reached out and rested a hand on the woman's back. The young mother may not accept her comfort, may even be angered by it, but she had to try.

At first there was no change in the woman's demeanor. No lessening of the heart-wrenching grief. Hannah stroked across the crying woman's back, her fingers finding the steady, circular rhythm that her mother had always used to soothe her.

After long minutes, the woman's tears began to ease, shifting to dryer sobs. Finally, she glanced at Hannah with swollen, blood-shot eyes, then reached for the blanket covering Itu.

Instead of shifting the top around her arms, she grasped the bottom and raised it to reveal the empty place where the girl's leg had once been. The leather bandage and newer poultice still wrapped the stump at her knee.

Her mother motioned across the area, and a moan slipped from her, followed by another sob, this one soaked in a fresh round of tears. Understanding swept through

Hannah. She *was* crying for a loss, but not the passing of a life. This was grief for what might have been. The death of her dreams for her daughter—hopes that included two working legs.

Hannah slipped her arm around the woman's shoulders, this time moving closer to lean into an embrace. She could only imagine the pain of this mother's heart—not for herself, but for her child.

If Hannah could tell her how desperately they'd tried to save Itu without removing the leg, she would. If she could describe the delirious fever and awful mangled limb, maybe the woman would understand how necessary the loss had been. But maybe knowing those things wouldn't really help.

Maybe the only true aid she could give was her comfort. A comfort that spread across languages and skin colors. A comfort that stemmed from Christ's love to her, a love she longed to share with this sister.

And so she held her, with tears slipping down both their cheeks and her heart lifted in prayer.

Nathaniel's stomach growled endlessly through the next day, but the tiny meals their captors offered were the least of his worries.

The man who he assumed was Itu's father seemed to grow more restless as the afternoon passed, striding in and out of the lodge with a thunderous glare pinned on his face.

He rarely gave Nathaniel a passing glance, but every time the man approached his wife by the girl's bed pallet, the glare he pointed at Hannah made Nathaniel's blood boil.

Did the man blame Hannah for his daughter's sickness? She'd done everything she could to help Itu, exhausting herself day and night, traveling for days with very little food, risking her reputation and likely angering her family. She didn't deserve this man's anger.

If anyone was to blame, it was this Indian brave for taking the girl away from the medicines she needed. But Nathaniel couldn't tell him that. Nor would it be wise, given their current situation as captives.

But he'd be watching the man. And he wouldn't leave Hannah's side when this Indian with the death glare was nearby.

He forced his attention away from the father to where Hannah was changing the poultice on the girl's amputated leg. "How is she?" Itu's mother had finally started leaving her daughter's side for a few minutes at a time, and she was gone now, so he didn't worry about keeping his voice as quiet as before.

"I think her fever's coming down." As Hannah spoke, Itu's eyes flickered open. "There you are, sweet thing." Hannah crooned to the girl as she dipped her hands in a wash pail to clean them, then focused her attention on the child's face, brushing the hair from her forehead.

"How do you feel?" Nathaniel's voice sounded husky in the quiet. He reached to tweak the toes of Itu's good leg that rose up under the blanket.

She gave a sleepy smile and mumbled some words.

"Are you ready to eat something?" Hannah glanced around, then moved toward a stack of pemmican sitting on a bark plate near the fire. She'd been allowed more movement than him, mostly because she needed to prepare the teas and poultices.

Maybe he should take over that responsibility from her. It would give him something to do at least. But then, maybe Hannah appreciated the chance to keep her hands active, too.

While Itu munched tiny bites of the pancake-like food, he entertained her with a song he'd sung to her back at his cabin. "Oh, where have you been, Billy Boy, Billy Boy?" The lyrics were nonsensical, probably something he'd learned from the soldiers on watch when they were out on a campaign. But the line that struck him in the chest just now was one he'd never given a thought to. "I have been to seek a wife, she's the joy of my whole life."

He glanced sideways at Hannah as he sung the words, catching the stiffening of her back before she handed the girl another bite to eat. He'd told Hannah he loved her, but he hadn't actually asked her to marry him. He couldn't until they were free from this place. Yet he planned to. Did she realize it? Should he tell her?

Not yet. The last thing he wanted was for her to be self-conscious around him. And he didn't want to get her hopes up in case… Well, he *would* get them out alive. He had to.

God, I'll need your help, though.

235

Hannah awoke in darkness again, but this time she couldn't place the sound that stirred her. She'd been trying to sleep lightly so she would hear if Itu needed her, yet nestled against Nathaniel made her want to forget about the unknown noises around her and stay tucked in his warmth and strength. She scooted away from him and pushed the blanket aside so she could rise and check Itu.

She shouldn't sleep next to Nathaniel like this. She knew it. Yet his hands were still bound and they were surrounded by chaperones, although not as many as the night before. And the protection of Nathaniel's nearness was one of the only comforts that helped her sleep.

Another sound drifted to her. Someone was up, over near the fire. Thick darkness still showed through the opening at the top of the tipi where the lodge-poles met and the smoke escaped. Whoever she heard must be adding more wood to the fire.

She kept herself still so she didn't draw the person's attention. Itu's mother seemed to regard her with a softer look after their shared moments the night before. But the father...the way he looked at her made her want to hide behind Nathaniel.

But she couldn't afford to show that kind of fear, so all she could do was pray for the Lord's protection and do her best to help Itu mend.

There was no doubt in her mind—

A hand pressed hard on her mouth, stilling her thought. The man's knee pushed into her arm, pinning it to the ground. His other hand grabbed her other arm before she could think to move it.

She tried to scream. Tried to jerk away, closer to Nathaniel, but the man pushed her hard to the dirt floor. She could only draw a shallow breath through her nose, but the stench of unwashed flesh nearly sent bile surging up her throat.

All she could see of his face was loose black hair hanging long, drowning his features in shadows as he loomed over her. Yet, she knew without a doubt this must be Itu's father. The anger in his grip matched the venomous looks he'd been sending her all day.

In a deft movement, he jerked her upright, keeping a grimy paw over her mouth. Terror surged in her chest as he lifted her like a cloth doll. She kicked out, trying desperately to touch Nathaniel. To alert him of her danger.

But her attacker was too swift. He swung her around and strode toward the lodge door. She reversed the direction of her blows, kicking his leg with her heels. Bending her knees to strike as high as she could.

Nothing slowed him.

The beast carried her outside, between the lodges, then through another row of lodges. No matter how much she struggled, the man carried her like a loaf of bread. So she turned her focus on watching where he was taking her. What did he have planned? Surely the other Indians didn't sanction whatever awful thing he intended, or he wouldn't have stolen her away in the dead of night.

Fear wound a tight knot in her belly as he carried her outside the camp, across a stretch of grass, and into a copse of trees lining the base of a mountain. She tried to bite at his hand, anything to throw him off balance so she'd have a chance to get away. Or at least to fight.

But nothing stopped this bear of a man. Her struggles seemed to only anger him more as he hauled her farther away from any chance for help.

At last, he dropped to his knees and tossed her on the ground, face up, with his hand still pressed firmly to her mouth. Her hands were free now, and she clawed at his arm to rid herself of his hold.

He mumbled something she couldn't understand, then sprang on top of her, straddling her and pinning both of her arms with his knees.

The feeling of him sitting on top of her sent a flood of terror through her chest. Did he plan to take advantage of her? What other reason would he have for bringing her so far from camp?

Oh, God. Help me. This wasn't supposed to happen. She was here to help his child. How could he do this thing?

She fought to free herself from him, but the man was like a granite boulder pinning her down. She was already struggling to breathe through the thin opening at her nose, and now with the weight of him and the panic pressing hard on her chest, she could scarcely draw any air into her frantic body.

With a quick movement, he pulled his hand away and pressed a leather strip to her mouth. The action was so sudden, and she had so little breath, she didn't have time for more than a gasp before he jerked the gag tight, twisting her head to the side so he could tie a knot tight enough to stop her blood from flowing.

Her mouth ached, but that was nothing compared to the awful truth of what he must be planning next. She had to stop him. *Lord, give me the chance. Get me away from this man.*

When he was satisfied her mouth was bound, he sprung to his feet in a lithe motion, taking her hands with him and pulling them over her head. Now that he no longer sat on her midsection, she took in cleansing breaths, as deep as her gag would allow.

But when the coarse leather pulled tight around her wrists, her mind finally sprang to life. He was taking away her chance for freedom. She raised her legs to kick, but there was no way she could reach him unless she spun herself around. Twisting, she bent herself over and drew her legs up to strike him where he bent over her hands.

He must have been too focused on trussing her up to see the blow coming, for she hooked her feet on his leg.

But like a solid oak, he didn't budge, only dropped an arm over her legs to hold them next to him.

Fury surged through her, overtaking all fear. She kicked with every bit of strength she had, both to free her legs and to do damage to this brute.

He grunted, then released her feet and stepped away in a single motion. The rope around her hands tightened, stretching her arms far over her head. He must be tying her to a tree.

Terror flooded back a hundred-fold. She writhed, turning herself over and pulling her knees up under her. She'd stop this ogre or die trying. With her feet still bound, it took extra balance to stand, but he wasn't watching her as he made quick work of knotting the leather cord around a tree.

This might be her only chance.

She dove forward, clasping her tied hands and aiming her fists at his head. It was an all-or-nothing leap. If this didn't slow him down, her only chance would be lost. Her aim was true, and she would have struck him full in the face had he not stepped back at the last second.

She landed across his arms. He must have planned the movement, for he hoisted her up, shifted back to where she'd been lying, then rolled her off his arms. She landed hard on her back, knocking some of the air out of her.

For a moment, she lay there, trying to collect her faculties. Trying to draw enough breath to still the desperation in her chest. Yet, nothing but freedom from this beast would ease her terror.

He bent beside a tree near her feet, then moved to her legs and pressed a hard knee to her right shin. His weight might have broken the bone, it hurt so badly. And the pain almost distracted her from the knife he now brandished. With a single flick, he cut the straps securing her ankles, then pulled her legs apart and tied a new leather cord around her left leg.

The feeling of her legs being spread, opening herself to his vile plans, even though her skirt still covered her, sent a new bolt of panic through her. She kicked hard with both legs, but only managed to move the one he was tying since the oaf still kneeled on the other.

She could do nothing to fight the strength of this madman. *God, you have to help me. Please!*

Chapter Twenty-Three

Lord, no!

~ Hannah

Why wasn't God doing anything to protect her? Surely he didn't want her to be assaulted like this. Her most sacred possession—her virginity—stripped away in such a ruthless manner.

Tears sprang to her eyes as her captor secured another cord around her final leg, then pulled the leather tight so she lay spread-eagle.

She'd never been so vulnerable. And there was nothing she could do about it. Hot rivulets of sweat rolled down her temples as she raised her heart in desperate prayer.

The despoiler moved to her right side, and as he raised her skirt, she couldn't help but think of Itu. This was the same leg that had been so mangled and was now missing. Did Itu ever feel this exposed as they worked over her wound?

Hannah pressed her eyes shut. Surely not, since the child had never been tied and gagged. *Lord, be with that sweet girl. Heal her, no matter what happens to me. And help Nathaniel.*

Her heart ached as she thought of Nathaniel. She'd had such wonderful hopes for a life with him. Would he even want her after this…tainting?

Would she survive what this man had in store for her?

She kept her eyes squeezed tight, trying to block out his actions. And it was working, for she felt nothing from him. No touch. No sound of his movement. She'd never known how easy it would be to remove herself mentally from a horrible trauma.

Then a sound broke through. Something like a whizzing. The ring of something striking wood.

"Stop!"

She jerked her eyes open at the man's voice. A familiar tone.

The Indian still hovered over her, still positioned at her exposed leg. Yet his attention was focused on a point above her. Beyond her.

She wanted to know what he was staring at. To see who had now entered her place of torture. Yet she couldn't take her eyes off her captor. This creature who'd been so indomitable just a minute before was now frozen.

Something had finally stopped his debauchery.

"Step away from my sister."

That voice. She twisted her head to see behind her, and the man standing in the shadows sent a frisson of shock through her.

Reuben.

Reuben Scott worked hard not to let his rage show as he pointed the business end of his rifle at the Indian. If he'd been five seconds later, the hatchet poised over Hannah might have been the death of her.

A sound from behind nearly pulled his attention toward the new attacker, but he could tell from the tread it was Simeon. His father.

"Reuben?" Simeon's voice was low, and the question in his tone meant he was still trying to make out the situation. And then his voice changed. "Hannah? Oh, God, help her."

"I don't think he's done anything yet. Cut her loose and use the straps to tie him up. Watch him." Reuben struggled for Crow words to question the Indian. The man was Hidatsa. Reuben knew that from watching their camp all day. But the two languages were similar, so he may be able to communicate with the snarling man. And there was always sign language, although that would require moving closer and lowering his gun—an act he wasn't about to do until this murderer was securely bound.

While Simeon cut his daughter loose, Reuben finally found the Crow words to ask the Indian, "What were you doing to her?"

It had been fairly obvious the way the man was positioned to strike a hard blow with his tomahawk, but

Reuben wanted to hear the man's intentions from his own mouth. Thank God he'd arrived and knocked the weapon out of the man's hand with a well-place fling of his knife. And the next question would be, *why?*

The man spat on the ground and looked like he wouldn't say anything, just glared a menacing look at Reuben. Then he did speak. A string of Hidatsa Reuben would never be able to pick out.

He positioned the rifle so it was perfectly aimed at the man's heart. "Speak in Crow." There was a good chance this fellow knew the language. He just needed a bit of encouragement to accommodate.

Simeon had Hannah loose now and moved behind the Indian to tie his hands. The man tried to jerk away, and might have succeed as strong as he was in his youthful prime, but Reuben took a step closer with his rifle.

The Indian's glare turned harsher, sharp enough to cut iron. But he stopped struggling and allowed Simeon to bind his wrists.

"Better put two straps around him. He's a strong one." Reuben switched to English for his father.

Hannah had come to stand beside Reuben, well away from the man who'd held her captive. "What are you going to do with him?" Her voice held a bit of quiver that proved her nerves hadn't quite settled. And he couldn't blame her.

"I think we should tie him here 'til we get some answers. Then decide what next." He didn't expect to grant this stranger much leeway, but every man deserved a proper trial if there was time.

Simeon nodded as he backed the man to a thick pine. "I agree."

"Hannah?" Emma's voice came from the shadows behind them. She'd been sleeping back at camp when he'd heard the sounds and woken Simeon to let him know he was going to investigate.

"Mama?" Hannah whirled and stepped into her mother's arms.

Reuben forced his focus back to keeping the Indian sighted down his rifle barrel. He couldn't let up until he knew for sure the man was bound securely. Even then, Reuben wouldn't be turning his back on him.

While he and Simeon worked to secure the man, he could hear the running conversation between the two women.

"How did you all get here? How did you know I needed help?" Hannah's voice still held a bit of a daze.

"We've been following your trail for two days. We found the Hidatsa camp this morning and have been watching for the right time to get you and Mr. Peak out. As for tonight, I'm certain that was God's mercy. Reuben heard noises and went to investigate." The control in Emma's voice gave way a bit. "Oh, Hannah. What happened? Did he do anything to you?"

"I'm not hurt, Mama. Reuben arrived before he could do more than lift my skirt."

Lift her skirt? It had certainly looked like the man had more than sexual plans for her. He'd been about to chop into her with a tomahawk.

Simeon tied the last knot securing the Indian to the tree, then stepped back. Reuben stood before the Indian, his rifle still in hand. Now was the time for answers.

He leveled his gaze on the blackguard and switched to Crow. "What were you doing to my sister?"

The man raised his chin in defiance.

Reuben moved closer, aiming the rifle squarely at the man's chest. "What were you doing to my sister?"

For a long second, the stranger did nothing. Then he spat in Reuben's face and spoke in Crow. "She needs her leg cut off like she cut my daughter's leg. I do this thing."

It took a second for him to process both the words and their full meaning. Could this be...? "You are Itu's father?"

The man gave a proud nod, his eyes still full of malevolence. "She destroyed my daughter's life. I destroy hers."

Destroy. He looked to Hannah and switched to English. "Has Itu died?"

She clutched a hand to her chest, her face losing color. "No. I...she's doing better. At least, when I checked on her a few hours ago."

Reuben turned back to the man and changed to Crow again. "Your daughter lives. She is not destroyed."

He shifted his leg. "Her life will never be the same. Is destroyed."

Frustration surged through him at the narrow-mindedness in the man's words. "My sister did not cut off the girl's leg. Your daughter came to us so wounded she

247

would have died. Removing the leg was the only way to save her life. She's healing now. She will live and learn to play and be happy as she ever was. Your daughter is strong inside." Which was more than he could say for this butcher.

Reuben gave the man a chance to respond, but he only received the same proud glare. At least Reuben had his answers now.

Turning to face the others, he tried to find the words to gently explain what the man had been on the verge of doing. Just the thought of him hacking off Hannah's leg made his stomach churn. She could have easily bled to death if the wound wasn't treated immediately — and correctly. And from the hatred in this Indian's eyes, Reuben was pretty sure the man wouldn't have spent much effort to cauterize the blood vessels and dress the wound.

Swallowing down the bile rising to his throat, Reuben looked at his new sister. "Hannah, when I found you, he was standing over you with his tomahawk raised. I thought he'd planned to kill you. His position was odd, more toward your legs than your neck or scalp, but my only focus was stopping him." He let out a breath. "Now I understand why." He didn't want to tell her this. Everything in him revolted against speaking the words.

Hannah stepped toward him. "What, Reuben? What did he say?" Her voice was sure now, her face solid. This new sister of his was a strong woman.

So he spoke plainly. "He said he planned to cut off your leg, so your life would be destroyed the way his daughter's life has been."

Hannah sucked in a breath, and he was pretty sure Emma and Simeon both did, as well. "He..." She seemed to struggle for words. "But she's alive."

Reuben nodded. "I told him that. Told him she was a strong young lady who'd grow up to play and thrive just like the other children. He's pretty set in his anger, though."

"Hannah, we need to get you out of here." Simeon strode forward, then paused to look from Reuben to the Indian. "What should we do with him?"

Before Reuben could form a good answer, Hannah spoke. "I'm not leaving without Nathaniel. And I need to make sure Itu's mother knows how to care for her."

Her father turned to her. "I'm not gambling with your life over that girl's. She's with her people now. They have the herbs you brought. It's time we went home."

"I'm not leaving Nathaniel." Her voice held a hard edge. A determined set to match the jut of her chin.

Simeon simply stood looking at her for a long moment. He had to know they couldn't leave Peak here at the mercy of the Indians.

And there was still the matter of what to do with Itu's father. If they left him tied to this tree, his people would find him, they'd let him go, and he'd be able to exact his revenge. Reuben could kill him, but that would likely have his people out for revenge. He may have intended to maim or kill Hannah, but taking a life was not something to be done lightly.

The best thing would be to talk to the rest of the camp. If they were decent, as most Indians were in the peaceful tribes like Hidatsa, they'd see the man's evil and punish him themselves. That would probably be the best way to get Nathaniel out, too.

Reuben focused his attention on his father. "I think I have a plan. But start praying, because we're going to need Divine intervention for this to work."

Nathaniel struggled to force his eyes open.

He could hear the activity around him, which meant he should have awakened long ago, yet his eyelids felt weighted. Almost as if something had been laced in his food to make him sleep.

That thought jerked him awake, although he still had to work to make his mind come alive. He sat upright and took in the room. There were more people in here than there had been the day before, milling about and talking.

He finally spotted Itu's mother, who was standing to one side, wringing her hands as a man spoke to her.

But the one person he wanted to see the most wasn't there. Where was Hannah? His chest constricted as he searched again. She'd only been allowed to leave this lodge for short trips to relieve herself. As had he. And each time they'd been heavily guarded.

It was possible that's where she was now, but the general unrest in the room made his gut clench. Had she been taken somewhere? Surely she hadn't escaped on her own, not without at least saying something to him.

His gaze slid to Itu. Had she worsened, and they'd taken Hannah away as punishment? But even before that thought could plant itself, he pushed it away. The girl's eyes were open, and her face seemed to have a bit more color than before.

He crawled toward her. "Where is Hannah?" Maybe he should have started with a smile and a good-morning, but the tightness in his chest was swelling quickly into fear. Something wasn't right, and if Hannah was in danger, he had no time to waste.

The girl's brows drew together in a puzzled look. "Hannah?" She knew who he spoke of, he was pretty sure. Did that mean she didn't know where Hannah was either?

Itu looked over Nathaniel's shoulder and spoke a string of sounds to someone behind him. He turned to see her mother return a flurry of words, accompanied by something that resembled a shrug.

Surely *she* knew where they'd taken Hannah. But Itu didn't look satisfied with the response, and volleyed back more words he couldn't understand. The two went back and forth, then Itu worked her arms up underneath her as if she planned to get up.

The girl's mother rushed to her side and held her down, an easy feat since Itu was so weak. She let into the child with a string of words that sounded an awful lot like chiding.

251

While she hovered over her daughter, Nathaniel turned to study the activity around him. Whatever the woman had said, Itu was worried about Hannah now too.

He had to find her.

Chapter Twenty-Four

My worst fear…

~ Nathaniel

If Nathaniel could get the ties off his hands and legs, or at least his legs, he could possibly slip out among all this movement. The only things he could see that would be sharp enough to cut thick leather were the knives sheathed at the waists of the men in the lodge. Getting one of those would be harder than escaping.

Could he creep to the fire and burn the strap? It was tied over his boots, so his skin probably wouldn't scald in the process. His boots surely would, though. The cord was pulled so tight it dug into the thick leather of his shoes, making it impossible to remove the boots.

Burning the ties may not work, but that looked to be his best option. He had to try it.

Crawling across the floor would draw attention, so he pushed to his feet and tried to shuffle forward. Surely anyone who glanced his way would know something was up, but the Indians seemed so preoccupied they might not notice him scooting around the edge of the lodge.

He'd only made it two small steps before a brave poked his head into the lodge and shouted a few quick words.

Everyone in the room surged toward the door, one stocky woman nearly knocking him over. A glance around proved that even Itu's mother had gone to stand in the open doorway, peering outside at something.

This was his chance. He shuffled toward the fire as quickly as he could. Hopping would have been faster, but Itu's mother stood where she could still see him if she turned, and he didn't want to pull her attention away from whatever she was staring at outside.

He had an awful feeling the commotion had to do with Hannah, but he wouldn't be much help to her until he could get his hands and feet free.

The fire singed his skin as it also burned the leather holding his wrists. An acrid odor rose up to sting his nose, and his arms stung as if they'd been nicked by bullets, but that was the least of his worries. The only thing that mattered was getting to Hannah.

With his hands free, he tried once again to untie the knot at his boots, or to get one of them off. The leather was pulled so tight, his feet had tingled for the first day. He'd tried to keep wiggling his toes so the blood would flow through, but he could barely feel them now.

And there was no getting his boots off with the ties in place.

He sat down and held his feet over the fire. It was hard to get the positioning right so the flame licked at only the strap, and again, the acrid smell of burning leather filled the air. At least he could only feel heat, not a direct burn on his ankles.

Finally, the cord popped free.

His legs split apart, and a pain shot up the outside of his thighs. He lowered his feet to the ground, trying to wiggle his ankles to wake things up.

They wouldn't move. At least, not at first.

When he was able to shift his right ankle, fire lurched through the joint. He sucked in a breath. He didn't have time for this. He had to get on his feet and see what was happening outside.

A hush had fallen over things out there, although he could hear the sound of a man's voice. He couldn't understand the words, but something important was taking place.

Hannah needed him.

He worked up to his knees, then positioned his right foot underneath him. He could push through the pain, but the minute he tried to put weight on the limb, his ankle buckled.

Biting back a growl, he tried again. The joint held a second longer than before, but it wouldn't bear his weight. He tried the other leg, but had the same result. Maybe they just needed time for the blood to flow smoothly again.

He crawled toward the open lodge flap, being careful to stay on the side near where he and Hannah had slept. If someone entered, he could crouch back and pretend to be bound if he needed to. The blanket could also help shelter him.

Itu's mother had left the doorway, and he could still hear one or two men's voices talking in strong tones a little distance away. He had to see what was happening.

A glance back at Itu showed a worry line creasing her normally smooth brow. She nodded, as if to encourage him onward.

Slowly, he poked his head out of the lodge, watching for any sign of people. No one moved about in the path between the tents. Beneath the sound of the men's voice was a faint murmuring, like that of a crowd talking in hushed tones. Had the whole camp gathered to see what was happening?

He had to crawl completely out of the lodge before he saw the outer fringe of people. He'd be extremely vulnerable in this position if anyone came running back to the lodge, but he'd just check to see what was happening, then move to a safer place.

Keeping himself as low as he could, he peered around the edge of stretched animal skins. A crowd of people stood flocked together. The camp was on a small slope, so he could just barely see the men standing a little apart from the others up the hill.

One had the shiny black hair of the Indians. The other wore a hat, much like the one Reuben had worn. Could it be? Had Reuben come to free Hannah? Maybe he'd stolen her away in the night, and that's why there had been such turmoil. But if he'd gotten Hannah out of the camp, why was he back?

Surely not for Nathaniel. As much as the thought sent a rush of relief through him, he'd take Hannah's freedom over his own any day.

He needed to stand so he could see them better. Grabbing onto one of the lodge poles, he worked his feet back under him. This time, the ankles bore weight a little better. Not strongly, but he could probably stand if he leaned against the post. He had to grit his teeth against the pain, but he finally made it mostly upright.

Thank you, Lord.

And as he focused his gaze on the men in the distance, the man wearing the hat did look to be Reuben. And there was another shorter figure beside him. Nathaniel could only see the top of the person's head, but it sent a surge of blood pumping through his veins.

Hannah. He'd recognize her pretty honey-brown hair and the beautiful line of her forehead anywhere.

Reuben was speaking, and he and Hannah were almost surrounded by Indians, but none of them seemed especially angry.

Then a roar surged through the crowd, and people turned to their neighbors with angry looks and expressive hand gestures. Nathaniel stiffened, letting go of the lodge pole. His feet would bear his weight now, but he wasn't sure he could walk a normal stride, much less run.

But if Reuben and Hannah needed him, he'd force his body to do what he had to.

He needed a weapon. Maybe one of these other lodges would have spare knives or clubs stored inside.

He eyed the nearest one, but he'd need to cross the opening between the tipis, and people would be able to see him. Probably best done crawling to keep himself low.

But just as he dropped to his knees, the people turned en masse, shifting so that a path opened up in the midst of them. Nathaniel jerked backward to keep from being seen. But he peered just far enough into the main walkway so he could see what was happening.

Hannah and Reuben were walking through the divided crowd. She looked worn and tired, and a bit disheveled. But whole. Walking of her own accord. No longer bound.

And absolutely beautiful.

Beside her strode Itu's mother, and behind them, several braves marched. Guards to make sure they didn't escape? *Lord, no.* If Reuben was here, then that meant somehow, Hannah had been free. Why had Hannah come back? Itu seemed to be mending more each day, so surely she wouldn't have returned just to care for the girl. Especially since she knew he was still here to continue the treatments.

Lord, don't let her have returned for me. Please. He'd never forgive himself if she or Reuben were hurt because of him.

The procession was coming nearer, clearly marching toward this lodge where he'd been staying. Should he get back inside and pretend to be tied still? That might be his best chance to free them all when the Indians weren't quite so stirred up.

He scrambled for the lodge door, walking mostly on all fours to get himself inside. He'd barely sat and covered his hands and feet with the blanket when Itu's mother stepped in. She held the flap aside for Hannah to enter, then Reuben. At least they weren't being handled roughly like before. And neither were tied.

Hannah's gaze flew to him as she stepped inside. Every part of him wanted to run to her. Well, every part except maybe his feet, which still burned like a fire raged inside them. It took all his willpower not to jump up and pull her into his arms.

She walked forward with measured steps and knelt beside Itu. The girl grabbed Hannah's arm as a smile lit her face. "Han-nah." The word was choppy but adorable.

"Oh, Itu." Hannah bent low and wrapped the girl in a hug. He couldn't see either of their faces, but he had a feeling Hannah was fighting off tears. His own eyes were stinging a bit at the thought of leaving this sweet girl behind. She wasn't theirs to take with them, but she'd always have a place in their hearts.

Could there ever be a way they could come visit her? *Lord, that might be too much to ask, but...*

Reuben crouched next to Hannah but near enough to Nathaniel that they could share a quiet exchange. Nathaniel wasn't about to miss the chance, but he kept his voice low. "What's happening? Can you get Hannah out of here?"

Reuben kept his gaze on the tender scene of woman and child. "They're letting all three of us go as soon as Hannah shows the girl's mother how to care for her."

Nathaniel sucked in a hard breath. All three of them? How had Reuben accomplished it? Everything in him wanted to ask the questions aloud. To find out where Hannah had been that morning. And why Nathaniel had been drugged to keep him sleeping, for he was fairly certain that's what had happened.

He held his tongue, though.

While she kept a hand on Itu's arm, Hannah turned to the girl's mother and pulled her into a halting exchange, with Reuben acting as interpreter. Together, they removed the bandage over the girl's stump and changed the poultice, then applied a fresh covering. The wound didn't look nearly as crimson and festering as it had the day before.

Thank You, God, for healing this child. For he had no doubt only a Divine hand could have accomplished so much in only these few short days, given how sick the girl had been when they arrived at this camp. And orchestrating their safe release from captivity? Not even Reuben Scott could accomplish that without God influencing the hearts of these Indians.

And what of Itu's father? Nathaniel hadn't seen him in the crowd or the procession. He certainly wasn't here in the tent now.

Lord, don't let him be up to no good. The moment he could speak freely to Reuben, he needed to spread the concern so they could both watch for an attack. He could just imagine the angry father lying in wait for them on their way back through the mountain wilderness. Now that Hannah was imparting instructions for Itu's care to the girl's mother, there was no reason for the man to keep them alive.

He forced his attention back from the swirling thoughts to see what Hannah was doing now. She seemed in earnest conversation with the Indian mother as they mixed dried plants for a tea. Although Hannah talked through each of her actions, naming the herbs as she selected each, the conversation seemed to take place more with looks and the gentle guiding of hands.

Somehow, these two women had bonded, despite the unspoken wall that had stood between them from the beginning. Did Itu's mother finally realize that the girl's leg had to be taken to save her life? Or maybe she was simply willing to put past grudges behind them for the good of the child.

Either way, watching the women interact seemed nothing short of a miracle, even the knowing smile the two shared when Hannah almost dumped the contents of the cup when she tried to stand.

Itu's mother took the tin cup from Hannah and moved to her daughter's side, helping the girl drink with the same gentle movements Hannah used.

Hannah scooted backward to allow them room. Yet he could tell by the slope of her shoulders the sadness she must be feeling. He slipped a hand around her back, and she leaned into him, resting her head on his arm.

An ache tightened his chest. If he could do anything to take this loss from her, he would. But it was right for Itu to be with her family. Especially when her mother so clearly loved her.

Lord, maybe You can find a way for us not to lose her completely.

Chapter Twenty-Five

Is this rending of my soul truly necessary?

~ Hannah

Hannah worked hard to hold her head high as she marched out of the Hidatsa camp, her brother on one side of her, and the man who'd so completely won her heart on the other.

If only her heart didn't feel like she'd left a piece of it back in that Indian lodge, cradled in the tiny fists of a brave little girl.

As Reuben led them through the trees, her mind wandered back to what Itu's mother had told Reuben about how the child had ended up in Nathaniel's barn. How she'd accompanied her father on a hunting trip, but things had gone terribly wrong when she stepped in the trap that broke her leg. How he'd ended their planned excursion, but had left her in the barn to rest out of the rain while he hunted for food they could eat the rest of the way back to camp. When he returned, Hannah had already carried the girl into Nathaniel's cabin.

So the man watched and waited. The presence she'd felt so many times, lurking in the trees, just out of sight. The thought of his leering face sent a shiver through her even now.

They stepped out of the trees and Reuben motioned them around the edge of a cluster of large boulders. The moment they stepped behind the shelter, her parents appeared with the three horses.

Her father stepped forward. "You made it." He gripped her arms and pulled her into one of the massive hugs she remembered from her little girl days. Emotion swarmed her eyes as she relished the warm strength of him.

"I'm sorry for worrying you." She barely choked the words loud enough for him to hear.

He pulled back and looked at her, his dark eyes as piercing as they'd always been. "I raised my girl with good, sound instincts, and I taught you how to follow them. I can hardly doubt you now." The lines at the corners of his eyes deepened. "I just hope those instincts don't always take years off my life."

My girl. No matter how many times she heard those words, they still had the power to melt her heart like candle wax in flame.

As tears leaked down her face, she reached up and pressed a kiss to her father's cheek. "You taught me well."

It wasn't long before they started on the trail. Nathaniel's horse hadn't been returned, so the five of them had to share the three animals her family had brought. Her parents rode together, and Nathaniel quickly commandeered her to ride in front of his own saddle.

Both her father and Reuben gave the man a long look, but neither said anything. She should pull her parents aside later and assure them that nothing untoward had happened between her and Nathaniel. It was probably a good time to hint that she hoped something very proper might happen between them in the future.

Namely, a marriage proposal.

Just the thought sent heat all the way up her back, and Nathaniel must have felt the shift in her, for he tightened his hold. She forced herself to relax, letting the tension slide out of her in a long breath.

And, tucked into the arms of the man she loved, she settled in for a long ride.

Nathaniel hadn't planned to seek Hannah out that evening as they were all setting up camp. In fact, with the dark looks her father and Reuben had been giving him all afternoon, he should probably keep a more respectable distance from her.

But after being so near her these past days, his entire being craved her presence. That beautiful smile that lit her from the inside. The way her melodic voice settled over him, soothing his tension.

And her touch. She had the power to fire his blood with only the brush of her fingers.

Was it too soon to ask her? Surely not after all they'd been through.

He could just see her willowy form through the trees ahead as she bent to pick-up firewood in the dusky light. He'd finished settling the horses, so he had time to help her with this task. Besides, there was still too much chance the Indians had gone back on their agreement to punish Itu's father for his planned violence. The man could be lurking nearby, waiting to kidnap her again.

Just the thought of that cad and his heinous actions sent Nathaniel's blood into a fresh boil.

Hannah looked up as he approached and gave him one of her smiles that eased a bit of the heat inside him. Then her look turned worried, probably from the expression on his face. "What's wrong?" She dropped the wood from her arms onto a pile of similar sticks she'd already gathered.

He forced himself to calm, to focus on Hannah as she was now, not on what might have happened. He shook his head and stepped nearer, a sudden need to touch her taking over. To feel for himself that she was alive and well.

She stepped into his arms when he opened them, as though she knew how much he needed her. He clung tightly, breathing in the softness of her hair, the warmth of her fully-alive touch.

Before he could stop himself, the question foremost in his mind slipped out. "Hannah, will you marry me?"

He could feel the intake of her breath. The way her body went completely still. Then she leaned back, forcing him to loosen his hold. Her eyes searched his face, and for once, her expression was impossible to read.

A weight pressed so hard on his chest, he couldn't draw breath. Did she not feel the same way about him as he did about her? Maybe he'd rushed things. What kind of woman wanted a proposal in the midst of a wilderness while she was gathering firewood? *Of course you should have waited, you simple-minded yokel.*

He released her and dropped to one knee, taking her hands in both of his. Her eyes widened even more, but he couldn't tell if it was from surprise or disgust. *Lord, let her say yes. If this be Your will, let her say yes.*

He inhaled a breath, trying to pull his scattered thoughts together. "Hannah, you're the woman I've been seeking for years now. In fact, I'd thought I'd never find you. Your heart, your passion, your strength and determination—they make me love you more every day. I don't have much to support you with right now. In fact, I'd planned to eat mostly meat and beans through winter. If you'd rather wait until next year to wed, I think it will be a little better. And Lord willing, our stock will grow each year after that. But I promise I'll do everything I can to provide for you. To give you the life you want."

She placed a finger on his lips, stilling his words. That couldn't be a good sign. Her eyes glimmered as if she was about to cry. Maybe because she planned to tell him no?

Desperation welled in his throat, and he almost moved her finger aside so he could try once more to make things right.

But then a laugh slipped through her beautiful lips. High and a little uncontrolled, but definitely happy. Hope surged in his chest to press down the desperation.

A tear slipped down her cheek. "I can't think of anything that would make me happier than marrying you." Another laugh slipped out. "I don't need much. With us working together, I think we'll have just enough."

He worked to assemble her words in his mind. To make sure she'd said what he thought. This was too important to get wrong.

She tugged on his hand, pulling him back up to his feet as she laughed again. "Did you hear me? I said yes."

She said yes. Joy and relief swirled inside him and he pulled her in tight, laughter bubbling in his own chest. "Thank You, God. Oh, thank You, God."

Epilogue

Only my Father above could orchestrate such a beautiful ending. Or rather, the beginning...

~ Hannah

*W*as she doing the right thing?

Hannah peeked through the slit in the door of Nathaniel's cabin at the crowd gathered outside. It was hard to believe how dear these people had become in the three months since she and her parents had arrived on Reuben's doorstep. A family much larger than she'd ever known.

Some connected by physical family bonds, others merely by heart ties.

Her gaze slipped to Cathleen, the new sister-in-law she already adored. She would be the perfect mother to the young life just beginning to grow inside her. Cathy held her niece, Amanda, on her hip while speaking to her elder brother and his wife. Doc Brian would always hold a special place in Hannah's heart for his tender, yet tough, care of Itu. And his wife, Claire, with her spunky personality and tenacity to care for anyone in need was the perfect match for him.

And then there was Doc Alex, Cathleen's younger brother, who now chased their three-year-old son, William, while his wife Miriam looked on, laughing. Her rounded belly was impossible to hide, but she'd stayed awfully slim from keeping up with their active lad.

Hannah could only stand in awe of the way these people had come together, all connected in an interweaving of lives that only God could have orchestrated.

Her gaze slid to her own father, tall and handsome in the best clothing he'd brought with him on this trip, speaking to Marcus, Claire's brother.

Except Marcus wasn't here merely for the pleasure of a trip into the mountains with his family, even though his beautiful wife, Lilly, stood nearby with their son and daughter.

A tingle slipped down her spine. As Butte's pastor, Reverend Marcus Sullivan was here to perform the ceremony.

Her wedding ceremony.

"Do you see him yet?" Mama slipped up behind her, voice gentle yet laced with the same anticipation churning inside her own chest.

Hannah shifted to see the area in front of the barn.

There.

The image of her groom, who was speaking with new friends they'd recently made, Gideon and Leah, sent a surge of love through her that settled all her roiling emotions. "He's talking with the Bryants. I think Gideon offered to sell some of his horses so we can start building up the herd."

We. The word felt so right, stirring an excitement inside her that made her want to step outside now, even though there were still a few minutes before the ceremony was planned to begin.

"Are you sure you want to go through with the wedding now, darling? We could wait until spring when your brothers and some of your cousins could come."

Hannah turned to face her mother. "Bring them in the spring. I'm sure I'll be ready for a visit. But this time is right for Nathaniel and me. I know it deep inside." She pressed a hand over her chest. "We're in this together. I need him and he needs me. He's the reason God brought me to this place at this time."

Tears lit her mother's eyes, as they had already done several times that morning. "I couldn't let you stay if I didn't agree with you. All the same, I can't imagine leaving without you."

Hannah stepped into her mother's arms, and the embrace raised a sting to her own eyes. More than a sting, but she did her best to swallow down the emotion. This was a day of joy, not sadness. "I love you, Mama."

After a long moment, her mother pulled back, sniffing and wiping under her eyes. "I love you too, honey. I suppose it's almost time."

Hannah inhaled a deep breath to settle her rioting feelings. She turned for one more peek through the slit in the door, finding Nathaniel easily now that she knew where he stood.

He must have finished his conversation with the Bryants, for he turned, and he gazed at the cabin wearing one of those gentle smiles she loved. He surely couldn't see her through the tiny peephole with the yard separating them, but her body responded as if he could. "Yes, it's time."

"I'll go tell everyone we're ready and send your father in." Her mother rested a hand on Hannah's shoulder.

She turned to offer a final reassuring smile, but Mama held out a bouquet of flowers. "I found some balsamroot just like we have at home. I thought you might want to carry them."

As Hannah took the bouquet of sunflower-like blooms, the familiar scent of home washed over her. This place wasn't so far from what she knew. The mountains, the trees, even the flowers had followed her here.

And now, mixed with the familiar, she would find new flora and fauna to discover. New adventures awaiting her each day. And the man God had created for her leading the way.

No matter what, she'd cling tight to their hands— both her new husband and her Heavenly Father.

Her mother leaned close and pressed a kiss to her cheek. "I'll send your papa in."

As Mama pulled open the door, a thought slipped into Hannah's awareness. "Wait. Has Reuben arrived yet?" Her new brother had left in the dark hours of the night to help a cow in need but had promised to be at Nathaniel's homestead by the wedding hour whether the animal had recovered or not.

Her mother poked her head out the door. "Yes, that looks like him now."

A sigh of relief swept through Hannah. No matter what, she wanted her special new brother to be here.

While she waited for her father to come escort her to her husband-to-be, she scanned the small room. Nathaniel had worked hard to put in the wood floor the past month, although she'd told him there was no rush. She would live happily under the stars as long as they were together. He also wanted to frame out a bed chamber on the backside of the cabin, but that would come in time.

They would have a lifetime to build the perfect home. A home that would grow as their family did, Lord willing.

A commotion sounded outside, and she stepped toward the door to see what was happening. But the partition swung open before she reached it.

Papa stepped inside, and for a long moment, he simply looked at her. His gaze slid down her best dress, which Cathleen had helped add lace to, then back up to her face. His eyes had turned glassy, and he stepped toward her. "You look beautiful, my girl. And so grown up." He pressed a kiss to her cheek, then stepped back as he cleared his throat. "There's someone outside who wants to greet you." His mouth curved in a gentle smile. "And not just that young man pacing in front of the preacher."

Someone else? Everyone she knew from town was already in the yard.

She took her father's arm and followed him out the door. The brightness of the sunlight struck her blind at first, and she shifted the flowers to the hand tucked through Papa's arm so she could shield her eyes with the other.

A horse's whinny drew her focus to the left, the direction of the main trail. Two horses approached. One was Reuben's familiar paint mare, and the other a tall chestnut that also struck a chord of recollection in her mind. The animal looked so much like Nathaniel's mare that they'd had to leave behind at the Hidatsa camp.

Riding the chestnut were two figures, one taller and one much smaller sitting in front. The matching black braids and tawny skin proclaimed them to be Indians, but it was the precious little face and the flash of a wide, beaming smile that sent Hannah's heart leaping.

"Itu!" She tugged her hand free from her father's arm and almost threw the flowers to him, then raised her skirts and ran toward the girl.

More than a month had passed since she'd seen that precious face, although she'd dreamed of the sweet child since then. Her heart sang a joyful tune as she neared.

But just before she flung her arms around the girl, a smidgeon of sense slipped through her pleasure, slowing her.

Itu's mother, Running Water, sat behind the girl. As much as Hannah wanted to pull the child off the horse and into her arms, this wasn't her daughter. She had to be respectful of Running Water's wishes.

A glance at the woman showed a smile brightening her face, too. Running Water extended a hand, and Hannah took it, pressing both of her hands around the woman's.

"Welcome." She poured all her thankfulness into the word. Into her gaze.

Running Water had brought Itu to share in this special day, and she couldn't have asked for a better gift.

The mother nodded, then motioned toward her daughter. Itu reached out with both hands and an even wider smile than before, and Hannah did what her heart longed to do.

Taking the child into her arms, she pressed her tight, squeezing her as hard as she dared. Now it was impossible not to cry, so she didn't even try to control the tears streaming down her face.

A warm hand pressed her shoulder, strong and reassuring. She didn't have to look back to know Nathaniel stood behind her, and she leaned into him. He wrapped his other hand around Itu, holding them both in his warm strength.

How right this felt, every part of it. Though Itu wasn't theirs to keep, she'd been the gift God used to bring them together. To show Hannah the true character of Nathaniel Peak and to plant the love that would continue to blossom in coming days.

Thank you, Father. My heart overflows with gratitude. When Hannah finally pulled away to look into the eyes of the man she loved, she could scarcely contain the joy welling within her.

Finally, she'd come home.

THE END

I pray you've enjoyed the finale to the Heart of the Mountains series! As much as I loved writing Nathaniel and Hannah's story and revisiting so many special friends, I'm always sad to say farewell...

But the sadness is softened because I get to share a new series with you! Hope's Highest Mountain *is book one in my new Hearts of Montana series (published by Bethany House, a dream come true for me!). I think you'll LOVE Ingrid and Micah!*

Here's a peek at the beginning:

Hope's Highest Mountain

Chapter One

My Darling Rachel,

You were everything to me. You still are. Don't ever forget that.

I saw a beaver today that reminded me of you. The creature paddled to the edge of the river and peered up at me through the water, just like that summer you learned to swim in the Ohio.

Your mama could barely pull you from the river to eat and sleep, you loved swimming so much. When you did come home, water dripping from your red curls, you always carried some treasure you'd gathered—smooth river rocks or a pail of tadpoles you planned to keep as pets. That was the summer you earned your nickname, sweet Ducky.

Mama didn't care for the title at first, but the name captured your personality so well, I couldn't help myself. Always swimming. Always smiling. My little Ducky.

I only wish I would have watched you swim more often instead of spending long days away from you and Mama. So much I missed. If I had it to do over again, I'd have kicked off my shoes and dove into the water with you. Played games to see who could reach the shore first or who could hold their breath the longest. I would have joined in any amusement you thought of, just to spend another marvelous hour with you.

I miss you every hour of every day.

Papa

****

October 1866
Montana Territory

"They say the last man who attempted this died in the doin'. Rest his soul."

A frigid gust of wind ripped around the freight wagon. Ingrid Chastain pulled her cloak tighter around her shoulders. She tucked her chin into her collar, blocking out both the icy air and the images their driver's morbid words conjured. This rugged cliffside might be as perilous as the old man described, but the staggering beauty of the mountains around them caused her chest to pulse, as though she was just now coming alive.

The mules plodded ever upward as the side of the mountain fell away on their left. It seemed a wonder this road could have been carved into the edge of such a jagged cliff. Every difficult step carried them higher, almost eye level with the majestic peaks surrounding them. This land possessed a strength she'd never imagined possible.

"Was the traveler properly prepared for the elements?" Her attention shifted back to the unlikely pair on the bench seat in the front of the wagon. Father, with his newly purchased fur coat, sat upright and confident beside their driver, a hunched gray-haired man in worn buckskins. Father spoke again, "Any endeavor worth doing can be harmful if not attempted correctly." Of course he would look at the story from the most logical approach.

Ingrid slid a glance at Beulah, their quiet maid, perched across from her. The supplies almost buried Beulah's ample curves but didn't hide her dark gaze swimming with worry. She looked away from Ingrid, down to their pet dog who'd nestled in her lap. Did she regret her determination to accompany Father on this trip of mercy? The gentle maid had been with them as far back as Ingrid could remember and had as tender a heart as any woman alive. When the desperate wire came, begging Father to send smallpox vaccines to an obscure mining town in the Montana Territory, Beulah had insisted on accompanying Ingrid and her father. There would likely be a need for nurses if the smallpox outbreak had spread.

Their driver didn't answer Father's words right away, merely hacked a raucous cough, then spoke to the mules as they climbed upward on the rocky trail. "Git up, boys." He added more encouragement with a flick of the reins. At last, he sent a sideways glance to Father. "I reckon' Angus Jones knew about these mountains as much as anyone. I 'spect he did as well as he could."

A moment of foreboding silence hovered in the air, mingling with the cloud of breath from their driver's words. "We've already passed the spot that did him in."

Father's shoulders relaxed. "Well then, Mr. Sorenson. We'll make it through just fine. I have faith in you, these mules, and especially in our Lord, who has promised to be our Salvation and Deliverer."

Mr. Sorenson didn't respond but hunkered down a little more, his elbows pressing on his legs. He coughed again, a rough bark this time, shooting another white cloud into the air.

"When we camp, I'll prepare a tea that will help your ailment." Father's voice hummed low, the tone he used with his patients.

Their driver leaned forward and flicked the reins on the mules' backs again as the brutal slope steepened. Ahead, the road bent in a switchback as it climbed toward the summit. The choice Mr. Sorenson made to use only a two-mule hitch to pull their substantial load made sense now. The tight turn would be a difficult angle for a longer rig pulled by more animals.

He guided the mules wide to take the turn, and another cough jolted the man's shoulders. He collapsed over with a ragged gasp.

"Sorenson?" Papa's shout came just as the driver dropped the reins. The leather straps bounced unguided against the wooden brace.

Ingrid's heart surged to her throat. She lunged forward, over the bench, scrambling for the leathers. Father grabbed Sorenson, and she slid her willowy frame under his arms as she closed her hands around the thick straps.

A mule let out a blood-curdling bray, and the wagon seemed to hover for a second. Or maybe a long minute.

Then the conveyance slid. The mule cried out again, this time sounding hoarse and strained.

The flap of Father's coat hindered her view of the animals. She clutched harder at the straps in her hands. Though panic stole her breath, she attempted to shake the reins, the way Sorenson had when urging the mules forward. "Git up!" Her voice didn't hold the strong command of their mule-whacker. Only shrill fear.

A loud crack splintered the air.

The wagon slid backward. Her grip tightened on the straps, clutching with every bit of strength. Though the wagon shifted beneath her, the animals hitched to the leathers didn't seem to move. The mules pulled her forward as the wagon slid backward, hauling her up on the bench between her father and their driver.

Father yelled. Someone screamed. Whether a man or woman, she didn't know.

Ingrid pulled the reins even harder, trying to end this madness. Her chest caught a hard blow on the front of the wagon—the footboard. She tried to brace herself against it, not finding purchase with her body.

But she refused to release the reins. Holding tight to the connection with the mules was their only hope of keeping them all from sliding down the side of the mountain.

Arms pulled at her. Or maybe it was the wagon pressing into her chest, wrenching her in two. She fought harder to keep her grip.

For a dizzying moment, she was rolling. Floating. Falling.

Something hard and heavy crashed into her leg. Then . . . blackness.

****

Micah Bradley forced one foot in front of the other as the icy wind surged along the mountain crag, buffeting his neck beneath his beaver-skin hat. He almost didn't notice the gusts anymore. Not much anyway. Except when the icy fingers snuck under his defenses.

A hoarse cry filled the air, stilling his feet mid-stride.

He strained to hear above the howling gusts. A mountain lion? Or maybe the eerie wail of wind sweeping around the rocks?

There, it came again. A mule?

No wagon train would dare venture through these mountains so near to winter. The first snowstorm appeared to be only hours away.

He plunged forward, angling higher up the mountain as he lengthened his stride. It must be another trapper. Yet something about the cry set the hairs of his nape on end and pressed him forward.

He rounded an outcropping of rocks, bringing the wagon road into view in the distance. A figure shifted on the trail. A man? His heart gave a leap. He'd not seen a person in weeks. He squinted to focus.

Two forms, actually. Animal, not people. One must be the mule he'd heard. Micah lengthened his stride. Where there were mules, there had to be men to handle them.

The animals lingered on the mountain road, waiting. But for what? No man moved around them. At least, none he could see.

Something was wrong. He could feel it in his bones. The same way he used to know his doctoring skills were about to be summoned, even before a pounding knock sounded on his door.

That had all been so many desolate years ago. Too bad the instincts hadn't died along with everything else he'd loved.

Get *Hope's Highest Mountain* at your favorite retailer.

Did you enjoy this book? I hope so!

Would you take a quick minute to leave a review?

It doesn't have to be long. Just a sentence or two telling what you liked about the story!

~ ~ ~

About the Author

Misty M. Beller is a *USA Today* bestselling author of romantic mountain stories, set on the 1800s frontier and woven with the truth of God's love.

She was raised on a farm in South Carolina, so her Southern roots run deep. Growing up, her family was close, and they continue to keep that priority today. Her husband and children now add another dimension to her life, keeping her both grounded and crazy.

God has placed a desire in Misty's heart to combine her love for Christian fiction and the simpler ranch life, writing historical novels that display God's abundant love through the twists and turns in the lives of her characters.

Sign up for e-mail updates when future books are available!
www.MistyMBeller.com

Don't miss the other books by

Misty M. Beller

The Mountain Series
The Lady and the Mountain Man
The Lady and the Mountain Doctor
The Lady and the Mountain Fire
The Lady and the Mountain Promise
The Lady and the Mountain Call
This Treacherous Journey
This Wilderness Journey
This Freedom Journey (novella)
This Courageous Journey
This Homeward Journey
This Daring Journey
This Healing Journey

Texas Rancher Trilogy
The Rancher Takes a Cook
The Ranger Takes a Bride
The Rancher Takes a Cowgirl

Wyoming Mountain Tales
A Pony Express Romance
A Rocky Mountain Romance
A Sweetwater River Romance
A Mountain Christmas Romance

Hearts of Montana
Hope's Highest Mountain
Love's Mountain Quest
Faith's Mountain Home

Call of the Rockies
Freedom in the Mountain Wind
Hope in the Mountain River
Light in the Mountain Sky

Made in the USA
Coppell, TX
26 December 2022

90768116R00173